JAMIE CARELA

Enchanted Transcendence

BEYOND THE SURFACE OF COLOR

"Sebastion Authur Robertson! Why are you so boring? You never get out of this dusty-ass bookstore and enjoy the night. You're still in your hundreds and have an eternity to go. Find a nice female and settle down."

Sebastion was only half listening to his older brother and sister as they gave their monthly speech on his life. He was a 600-year-old vampire who was different. All of his family and friends were ridiculously wealthy, as was he, but they lived very lavish lives. Bastian, however, was very intelligent and smart with his fortune. He was currently invested in technology, for example.

He always found the diamond-in-the-rough opportunities and was laser focused on them to make them shine. He was what you'd call rich rich. But he didn't live lavishly like his siblings. Instead, he opened a bookstore and lived in a small two-bedroom, two-bath room apartment above it. Bastian owned the building as well as the surrounding buildings as investment properties, but he was quite content with his simple life. That was until one summer day in the late evening when a stunning almond-colored beauty walked in.

She wore her sun-kissed golden brown hair in a curly puff on top of her head and simple, square, dark-framed glasses sat perfectly on her small, oval-shaped face. The way she moved through the bookcases, touching the spines of each book, aroused Bastian in a primal way. She moved like a soft breeze through a field. As Bastion watched the way she moved, he could almost imagine her touch on his body. He closed his eyes to try to picture her naked…

"Umm, excuse me?"

His eyes shot open. "Yes? … Umm … How may I help you?" He felt a little embarrassed, but kept his cool.

She was even more beautiful up close. Her eyes were the most beautiful golden hazel and her smile was flawless. Her skin looked like a warm copper or rose gold and just as smooth. "I was looking for a book on constellations and star formations. I can't seem to find any in the stacks." Her voice was like a song that was lost to the world but felt like home. "Do you carry such books?"

Bastion was so lost in her he couldn't form words, and then realized he hadn't replied. " Oh! Yes … umm… No, I'm sorry I don't have any on hand right now, but I could have them shipped here for you if you would like." Bastian was never one to be lost for words, but this magnificent creature standing in front of him has done it.

"Yes, please! I love the stars and reading the history of them," she said. "

Could I leave my number with you and once they arrive call me?"

"Absolutely," Bastion said, almost too fast to not be weird. "Sorry, yes. I will be in touch Mrs ?" his voice trailed off.

"Oh no. It's Ms. Or doctor. Dr. Autumn Scorpeno. Pleased to meet you." Bastion was much more impressed and intrigued. As she stuck out her hand to shake, he took it and immediately heat came over him.

"I'm Sebastian Roberston, owner of this little gem here."

Her skin felt like the softest silk he'd ever felt or spun. He'd never felt any thing so soft in all of his 600 years. "Well, I really enjoy little gems like this, Sebastian, if I may call you that. I love the smell of books and weird, nerdy things like that." Autumn laughed a little as she blushed at explaining herself to a stranger. Thank you again."

Bastion let her hand go as she turned to walk away. *Those curves...* Bastian thought. He couldn't help but stare at the way she moved her hips in those jeans, She was dressed for an evening of causal eating and reading at home, but dressed to kill nonetheless.

As Autumn was leaving the store, Bastian's brother Royce was walking past. Royce even stopped and did a double take. *DAYUM!* Royce mouthed to Bastian. "Who was that fine-ass thang?" Royce said, snapping Bastian out of his daze.

"She's mine," Bastion said blankly.

"What?"

Bastion blinked. "Ummm ... just a customer," he said as calmly as possible.

"Whatever man, you know I like my girls pale skinned, but that Nubian goddess there ... whew! She makes me rethink my female choices ... Dayum!

Bastion gave his brother a look. "B, don't look at me like that, I was just joking, chill. She is fine though."

"Yeah, she is," Bastion said, watching her walk out of sight.

* * *

"Nerdy stuff, Autumn! Uggh!" Autumn muttered to herself as she walked down the street. *You're an accomplished scholar,* she continued to herself. *The first black woman to lead the Neurology Department in St Louis and can't have an intelligent conversation with another person.* Autumn was down. When Autumn returned home, she immediately went into her bedroom and undressed. *"Maybe a hot bath, some wine, and Sade is what I need to release some pressure,* she thought.

As the bath water started to fill the marble spa tub, she sat on her king-sized bed. "Alexa, play The Sweetest Taboo by Sade." As the music began to play, Autumn found herself getting more relaxed. She poured herself a big glass of wine and slipped into her robe. She stopped as she walked past her floor-to-ceiling mirror. "Autumn, is that bookstore guy someone you'd let caress your golden curves? Would you let him touch and taste the sweetness between your thick-as-honey thighs? Would you take him into your sacred garden of Euphoria and hypnotize him with your rhythmic vibrations? Would you?" As Autumn was asking herself these questions, she didn't notice she had slipped her own fingers into her sweet spot and started to imagine what it would be like.

She thought about her encounter with the bookstore owner and felt herself getting wetter. He was tall, six-three at least, with dark hair. A very, very fine white man. He had broad shoulders and a vaguely foreign accent. He had seductive brown-red eyes behind dark-rimmed glasses. He looked very much in shape and umm …very well endowed. "Yes, ohhh, mmmm." "Dayum," Autumn said out loud. "Let me get in this tub before my water gets cold." As Autumn soaked, her thoughts went from riding that sexy nerd until he screamed her name to thinking that he wouldn't think twice about her.

"Girl, what we doing tonight? You need to get out. All you do is work, go to the gym, and read. Life is too short to not be out in these streets. We still young and sexy!" Autumn's best friend Sasha yelled at her on Facetime. "I know, but I don't have time," Autumn said tiredly.

"Itch! Yes, you do! We going out!" Sasha yelled. "I'm on this plane now so we can go to New Orleans for this Anna Rice party and we going to be lit!"

Autumn still looked shaken, laughed, and did just that. She packed, bought herself a first-class ticket, and left the comfort of her high-rise condo in the heart of Saint Louis for a weekend of debauchery with her best friend.

"B, pack your weekend bag, bro, we going out!" Royce burst into the bookstore yelling at Bastion.

"Nah, I'm good. I'm going to take care of these orders," Bastion replied.

"You mean you still haven't called Dr. Fineass yet?" Royce bothered his brother. "Why not? Didn't her books come in the next day?" Royce continued, laughing.

"Yeah, but what am I supposed to say? Just that her books arrived and that's it? That's lame." Bastion wracked his brain.

"Dude, you need to go on and relax. Come get lit with me this weekend. The mortals are going to the Anne Rice Vampire Ball in New Orleans. I want to taste all the fresh ass and blood coming through there." Royce was clearly excited about the event.

"I'm not looking for random ass, Royce," Bastion replied, giving him a push.

"Bro, you haven't smashed anyone new since April left."

"Royce, don't bring her up," Bastion said, getting upset.

"Chill, B. I'm just saying, I miss my best friend and little bro. Besides, Mira wants to check on the our estate there, too. She's thinking of doing some renovations on it."

"So, this is a family-work trip then?" Bastion asked.

"Yes," Royce said finally. "But it's with benefits, B. With benefits." Royce was almost begging at this point.

Bastion gave his brother a raised-eyebrow look, laughed, and finally agreed to go.

"Just for the weekend, though."

"All right!" Royce said, real slick.

As Bastion packed his bag, he smelled Dr Fineass's card. The scent of her still lingered on it. As he inhaled the scent and daydreamed of her. He replayed how beautifully curved and shaped she was. He remembered how her brown curls accented her almond-shaped eyes of golden hazel, her tiny nose and very faint freckles. Her perfectly round, soft, flawless face made him instantly hard. *I should call her when I get back.* As Bastion, Royce, and Mira boarded their private plane, Bastion was already far away in his mind, pleasing his exquisite creature until she fell asleep.

"Sasha, I just landed. Where are we staying? I need to know because you have really expensive taste. I'm not trying to stay around a lot of old-ass, rich white men, lurking and sweating us."

Sasha burst out laughing and said, "Autumn, how dare you? How dare you deprive them old men of all this Nubian Goddess golden-chocolate goodness? Girl! They might pay some bills," she continued, messing with Autumn. They both laughed as Autumn got into the rental car.

"We staying at the W. It's a block away from the event so in case it's lame, we can bounce. Autumn! Bitch! We made it!" Sasha ran up to her and gave her a big hug.

"Girl!, this room is lit!" Autumn said as she opened the door. It was a two-bedroom, two-bath penthouse suite. "Girl, how in the … better yet," Autumn said with a side eye and a slanted smile. "Who did you sleep with to get this room?"

Sasha spun around with a shocked and appalled face and giggled. "First of all, ma'am, Conner has some serious mouth game and I may have let him taste my goodies. Besides, he is a fine young thing and he was curious." They both burst out laughing and settled in for a fun-filled weekend.

*   *   *

"Damn, it seems like forever since we've been here," Royce glared at the huge English Victorian House.

"Yeah, we should come here more often, it's still so pretty. That old southern charm always makes me feel at home," Mira said as she opened the huge front doors.

"This place has so many memories," Bastion finally spoke as he walked into the foyer.

"Yeah B, you were only a hundred or so when we first arrived here, weren't you? Still a noob to being immortal and I'm pretty sure I smashed more chicks than you dated then, too," Royce boasted and laughed.

Bastion laughed too and punched his brother.

"You guys are still such idiots and so gross," Mira rolled her eyes.

"So … what do you think of the renovation ideas, Bastion?" Mira asked thoughtfully. "I trust your thoughts more than Royce because, well, it's Royce."

"Wow! Thanks for the confidence, sister dear," Royce said. Mira met him with an eye roll and pressed on through the house with Bastion.

"I think it's an amazing idea, Mira. I'm sure it will be incredible. You can keep the old-world charm and bring in a modern-day touch with amenities. It'll be dope," Bastion reassured Mira.

"Yeah, yeah. Look, everything will work out, big sis. You got this," Royce chimed in.

"So, little bro, let's get settled in so we can see what's up in these streets," Royce said as he hurried his brother upstairs.

"Ugggh, fine. It's probably going to be lame." Bastion went along reluctantly. What his brother and sister didn't know was that all he wanted to do was call Dr. Autumn "Fineass" Scorpeno. She was all he could think about. She haunted his thoughts. All he could during the trip to the house was imagine her naked almond skin in all its silken glory pressed against his skin as he pushed deeper into her ocean of sweet nectar. He could imagine how shallow her breathing would be as he tasted the sticky honey between her supple, quivering thighs. *Damn it*, Bastion caught himself rubbing his rock-hard member. "Whew, I need a cold shower real quick."

About an hour went by and Bastion was dressed and ready to hit the streets. He wore dark Marc Jacobs jeans and a smooth, coffee-colored button-down shirt with matching Marc Jacob shoes.

"Nice look, Bro! Let's hit the streets!" Royce yelled from the first floor. "Jones! Can you bring the phantom around? We stunting tonight!"

"Right away, sir," Jones replied before hurrying off.

*　*　*

"Dayum Autumn, all that time in the.gym got your body snatched, hunty!"

"Thanks, boo!" Autumn replied as she stepped out of the bathroom in her new red bandage dress from Fashion Nova, Cardi B edition. "Cardi herself would be proud!" Sasha laugh and squealed, "Eow!" They both laughed and continued to get dressed. "Girl, I love this vampire shit!" Sasha said as she finished her lipstick, checking her fangs to make sure she didn't get lipstick on them. "This shit makes me horny. ."

Autumn laughed, calling from the other bathroom, "Calm down with your fast ass. You know they aren't real, but to be honest if they were would they even fool with mortals?"

Sasha leaned out from her bathroom and yelled, "Girl who cares? As long as the slay with that immortal dick, I'm with it." Sasha finished lacing up her heels, stood, and posed in the mirror. They stood in their foyer to take a few Snapchat pictures before Sasha said, "Let's get lit with our fine asses!"

As they stepped into the elevator, Sasha winked and whispered, "Let's see who gets bit first." Autumn giggled as they went out for the night.

* * *

"Gentlemen, right this way. Welcome to our Halloween event. Your exclusive VIP table is already set and waiting." Royce had pulled out all the stops to make sure his brother had an unforgettable night.

"B, what you want to drink? They have really good O positive here," Royce said.

Bastion, getting settled into his seat said, "Yeah, I'll have one of those please."

The waitress turned to Royce and he was immediately aroused. "Damn, girl! Make that two, gorgeous."

She bit her lip and hurried away with a "Coming right up."

"I thought you said mortals threw these parties," Bastion wondered.

"Oh, they do, but vampires cater and host. Most mortals are so excited about the thought of being bitten or used as a sex thing for a real vampire that they don't care what it costs. Thank goodness for the blood drive," Royce laughed.

"Here are your drinks, gentlemen."

"Thanks, sweet thang. Come back later so I can taste you," Royce said, and the waitress nearly came as Royce ran his finger up her thigh.

"Damn bro," Bastion laughed. "Let her work."

"Fine." Royce tickled her clit real quick and let her walk away. He tasted his finger and said. "Yes, I'm going to tear her right on up."

Bastion laughed at his brother then turned his gaze to the first floor of the building. It was a sea of mortals and immortals alike. All had on masks and fangs, some real, some fake, but on this night it didn't matter.

The event was lit. About an hour into the party Bastion was finally beginning to relax and enjoy the night. Royce had taken at least three waitresses to the back and tasted them. "Bro, I don't know what these mortals in the south eat, but their blood and pussies taste like sweet potato pie or sun tea or something like that. Gosh damn!. . I might stay down here a little longer.." Bastion burst out laughing.

"It's so good to see you smile, little bro," Royce said sincerely.

"Indeed," Bastion said as he raised his glass. As Royce ordered more drinks, Bastion let his mind drift away to the good doctor. *What was she doing right now? Is she in bed with a book? Or at work helping someone?*

"Yo!" Royce yelled over the music and interrupting Bastion's thoughts. "B, look down there!"

Bastion gathered himself and looked over the balcony.

The DJ yelled into the mic, "I want to wish all the beautifully delicious ladies in here a Happy Halloween. May your dreams and fantasies be as wet as your panties tonight! Fellas! Let's make this happen."

"The DJ has some high expectations," Sasha yelled at Autumn.

Autumn laughed out loud and said, "Agreed."

"Did you see who I saw?" Royce yelled at Bastion as he stared wide-eyed into the crowd. "The ladies in red and purple dresses!"

"Nah, why?"

"Bro, let's go down and see what's up with them!"

Bastion grabbed his drink and said, "Bro, I'm good where I'm at."

Royce, getting annoyed, replied, "Whatever man, you trippin, I'm going to see what's up."

As Royce walked out, Bastion called after him, "Bro! It's not that it's …".Bastion stopped mid-sentence as he smelled something familiar in the air. "No way." Bastion got up to smell the air better and see where the scent was coming from. He looked over the balcony and saw Royce talking to a woman in a skin-tight purple dress. He stopped and smelled the air again. *No way, I'm this lucky.* Bastion remembered Royce saying something about a woman in purple, but also one in red. *Wasn't she with a woman in red?* Bastion's mind was racing. As soon as he thought it she moved in beside her friend. He inhaled the air one more time.

It is her! Bastion's mind and body froze as he recognized who the scent was coming from. *Holy Shit, it is her.* Royce pointed up to the second floor, where Bastion was standing and he all but froze. He was hypnotized in a trance as those golden hazel eyes shone like bright topaz against the dim lighting in the building. *Fuck!* Bastion thought. *What do I do? Be cool, Bastion, be cool.* As the door opened to their private section, Bastion stood up.

"Good evening, ladies."

Royce smirked and introduced him. "Ladies, this is my brother Sebastion. Sebastion, this is Sasha and Autumn. They are here for the weekend also." Royce did a little dance behind the ladies as they made their way to the couches.

"Very nice to meet you, Bastion." Autumn was stunned. *This is the same nerdy guy from St. Louis?* Autumn took in all of the deliciously dressed, sexy god. He didn't have glasses on and his clothing was tailormade from head to toe. His shirt was open at the collar and she could see she was right about him being very fit. His hair was pulled into a high man bun and *OMG, he has a goatee. Is this the same person?*

"Would you ladies like a drink?" Bastion asked, trying not to stare.

"Yes, please," Autumn said quickly. *Close your mouth!* she scolded herself as she caught herself staring.

"BIH, what's wrong with you? You act like you've met him before," Sasha whispered.

"BIH! It's because I have!" Autumn whispered back.

"Stop it!" Sasha laughed at her, as her attention was on Royce. Autumn sipped her drink slowly, as it was all she could do to not stare at Bastion.

Sasha and Royce were making out and laughing.

"I meant to call you. The books you ordered arrived at the store," Bastion said.

"It's okay. I'm sure you're busy with things and stuff. No biggie."

Damn it, Bastion, say something else! He thought, smiling his natural, fanged smile.

When Autumn saw his fangs, she immediately got wet. "Y - You look different. I mean you look amazing," She struggled to say.

"You as well." Bastion was already semi hard from her scent, and her being this close made it worse. "I love the red. It really accents … *the skin I plan to taste each and every inch of* your eyes." Bastion finally said.

"Thank you." Autumn was glistening. It was partly from the heat in the building, but also from being so close to the object of her fantasies. He could tell in the dimmest of light that she was blushing. He could feel the heat from her body radiating.

"Are you all enjoying your night?" The general manager came over to the table and asked.

"Yes, Gino, thank you so much. This event is epic."

"Thank you so much, Mr. Robertson" Gino replied.

As the night went on, Autumn and Bastion laughed, drank, and danced to all the music. At one point, Autumn looked into Bastion's eyes and they were ice blue. *Maybe I'm seeing things*, she thought. "Bastion?"

"Yes?" he said. After a few bottles of top-shelf alcohol, she was sitting in his lap, quite tipsy and happy, rocking away to the rhythmic beat.

"Can I kiss you?"

"What?" Bastion said, unable to believe he had heard her correctly.

"I know this is really forward, but you've been like my secret crush. For a while and at night I find myself touching myself when I think of you and I want to know what your kiss tastes like."

Bastion almost busted out of his pants as he listened to Autumn's drunken confession.

"Bastion," she said a second time.

"Yes?"

"I have fangs in, will that bother you if I kiss you with them?"

"Not at all, lass. I have fangs too," Bastion said.

Autumn leaned in really close to bastion and whispered, "You want to know a secret?"

Bastion was rock hard, and he could almost taste the beads of moisture from her neck. "Oh yes, please," he said.

"Sometimes, I imagine you as a vampire and you kiss all over my body and finally bite my pussy till I cum." Bastion's mouth fell open and Autumn grabbed his neck and deep kissed him for what seemed like forever.

When they finally came up for air, the event was ending and Gino was there to escort them to their car. "Maybe you'll call me," Autumn said as she and Sasha headed to their Uber.

Bastion, still high from the hypnotic injection of their kisses, was hurried to their ride and estate. "Well, gosh damn that was a fantastic night! We should do that more often," Royce said as he fell back onto the plush sofa.

"Yeah," Bastion said as he reflected on the night. He'd met that magnificent unicorn of a Nubian Goddess and practically felt all of her universe melt between her thighs. She wore that forbiddingly seductive red dress and it was just tight and high enough to slip his rock hard cock into her.

Bastion thought to himself as he felt his pants get uncomfortably tight in the groin area. *Fuck yeah.* "I'm going to take a long, cold shower" Bastion said.

"Don't you mean a hot shower, bro?" Royce asked as Bastion struggled to his bathroom.

"Nope, I need to calm down. . Night," Bastion yelled as he climbed the last step and closed the door.

"Night!" Royce replied.

"Boo! That Royce is a real freak! I mean he is super sexy and nasty! I was like, yes, absolutely. The fangs definitely did it for me," Sasha said as she slipped out of her dress. "He could get this work anytime! And he can keep his fangs in too. I am fa sho about that life!"

Autumn giggled at Sasha's replay of the last night's doings. "What's wrong, hun? You didn't have a great time? It looked like you did with Mr. Tall man-bun sexy thang."

"I did, but I know him from the bookstore."

"What?" Sasha sounded intrigued. "You mean that's the bookstore sexy nerd?"

"I mean, you're a nerd and cute," Autumn cut her eyes at Sasha. "I'm just saying … damn that's the same guy?" "Yeah!" Autumn said, finally glad Sasha was catching on. "OMG, I was stupid drunk and all on his junk last night and kissed him like it was going down." Autumn was slightly embarrassed and ashamed. "

I don't do shit like that, Sasha!" she said, on the verge of tears.

Sasha, saddened by her friend's stress, hugged her and said, "Honey look. You finally let yourself have a great time last night. So what if you were Cardi B when you're normally "Gabrielle Union? You had a great time and, honestly, I've missed your ratchet-hot ass."

Autumn burst out laughing and hugged her best friend. Autumn and Sasha had been best friends since their first years at Tennessee State University. Now they are both very successful professionals in their fields.

Sasha was a federal agent and now she's the district chief in the Saint Louis office of the Drug Enforcement Agency. Fifteen years of friendship and they had never let time or life get in the way of their friendship.

"You're right, you know," Autumn said to Sasha.

"BIH, I know," Sasha said as she blew her best friend a kiss. "Let's get some sleep so we can get up and get some mimosas."

"Are we going to eat breakfast?" Autumn wondered.

"Of course," Sasha replied. "Gotta have something to absorb the alcohol." They laughed as they finally went off to sleep.

*　*　*

"Well, good evening, gentlemen! I'm glad to see you bums had a great night," Mira shrieked. "Damn, Mira, why so loud?" Royce yelled, rolling over.

"I told you idiots I wanted to show this house tonight and look at you," Mira said, disgusted. "You still in your stank-ass clothes from last night! Y'all smell like stank thots! Royce, go wash your ass!" Mira continued to yell.

Fuck! I swear, Mira, for you to be a millennia old you sure act way older, Mooomm!"

Mira snarled at him, flexed her fangs, and smiled as she spoke ever so calmly, "We wouldn't have to renovate this estate if you had only done what Father and Mother asked you to do and kept the house up properly."

"Damn! Okay, Mira, shit, you're right okay? Chill," Royce tried to reason with Mira.

"Whatever Royce," she said as finally calmed down. "Just get showered, dressed, and ready for the showing." She was frustrated with her brother. "Bastian, are you dressed and ready for the showing?" she yelled up the stairs.

"Yes!, I'm ready," he said as he walked out of his room and down the stairs. He laughed at his brother who had run up the stairs for a quick shower and shave.

"That guy! I swear he is trying to kill me and we can't die!" Mira said as she hugged Bastion. He laughed at his sister's jokingly stressed position. "You look nice baby bro, I'm impressed."

"Thanks, sis," Bastion smiled. He was wearing a very nice burgundy Gucci suit. He matched it with a toffee colored shirt and matching shoes to complement the look. His hair was pulled into a low ponytail, freshly washed and smoothed back. He had cleaned up his goatee and shaped it with his sideburns tapered down to complete his bearded look. "You clean up pretty nice yourself, sis. You out here eating hearts and snatching souls?"

"Whew!" she winked. "Not in a while." Mira wore a very sexy but powerfully commanding Chanel pantsuit with her long red hair cascading over her shoulder in a very neat fish-bone braid. Her suit was midnight black with silver accents. "Royce Samual Robertson!" she yelled from the first floor. "What in the lost in space are you doing up there? Hurry up!" she yelled, frustrated. "We open the house in thirty minutes!" "Mira Louise! I'm coming down right now."

"Don't call me that!" Mira started arguing with Royce. Royce rushed downstairs in a hunter green Versace blazer with black pants and shoes to match. He also rocked a green and gold bow tie to complement his look. "Huh!. Very nice Royce! You didn't shave?"

"Damn, Mira! Let me live!" Bastion loved his brother and sister to the ends of the world. They were all each other had left since their parents were taken and executed. It was a touchy subject, one they never really talked about.

"Okay, this open house is just the beginning!" Mira squealed with excitement. "If we get enough investors interested, it could turn a multi-million-dollar profit for us!" The properties would still be in the family name, but other money will help keep it up to date and occupied, Mira gleefully explained to her brothers. "Bastion, you're amazing at pitching ideas, would you tonight? Your tech companies would get first dibs on modernizing the estate and it subsiaries if this goes how I feel it will."

"Sure, I'll give it a go."

"What can I do?" Royce asked.

Mira looked at her brother, rolled her eyes, and said, "Look pretty and sell the idea as best as best as you can."

Royce snarled at his sister and she snarled back.

"Chill, you guys. We're all in this together," Bastion was always the peacemaker between the two. "Let's get a drink and talk about how we approach this," he said, pulling his brother into the parlor.

"Yeah, you're right. At least someone sees my value!" Royce yelled at his sister's back. Royce cut his eyes at her as she walked away, flicking a middle finger at him. "She can be a real bitch sometimes, B," Royce said as Bastion handed him his drink.

"I know. But she loves you nonetheless, Royce."

"Yeah, I know, but she sure has a funny way of showing it."

"You also know she knows you are capable of way more then you are doing now."

Royce looked shocked at hearing this from his brother. "I am a CEO of one the U.S.'s biggest car manufacturers. We have the number-one domestic car sales in the nation and she's still not happy with that!"

Bastion could see his brother was getting bothered again. "Look, I'm extremely proud of you," Bastion reassured him. "She is too, bro, but I think it's more in how you're living personally."

Royce looking annoyed by this. "Such as?" he inquired.

Bastion felt wary about being in the middle. "Well, she feels you're using females as play things and random food sources, and posting on social media doesn't quite say 'I'm a focused and grounded individual', you know what I mean?" Bastion hoped he conveyed what their sister was trying to express without being too harsh.

"Yeah," Royce said flatly. "She wants me to live a boring as life like her and you."

Bastion was a little offended, but let it slide. "Sorry, bro, you're cool but neither one of you live your best lives and it's boring to watch. I'm 800 years old. I want to do as many females and things as I possibly can."

Bastion understood his brother's frustration and gave him a strong hug. "It's all good bro, maybe after your THOT phase you'll find The One." Bastion's line was an attempt to make Royce laugh and it did. "Yeah, she'll have to be a savage of a woman though. I need that that in my life."

" Indeed, bro," Bastion laughed. "Indeed."

As they were drinking and walking back into the front of the house, Mira announced the house was opening and directed them to take their places.

"She's like a ring master of a circus," Royce whispered to his brother. They both laughed quietly as they watched Mira drink her O positive wine and conduct the sea of potential investors into the huge house.

"Let the show begin," Bastion said to Royce as he took his cue from Mira to begin the presentation.

*   *   *

"Autumn, when you said we were going to see a historical thing I didn't realize you were looking into an investment project!" Sasha said, aggravated. "I don't want to work!" Sasha pleaded.

"Sasha! Come on. Stop it," Autumn laughed at her sweet, ridiculous friend. "You said you would go with me. Don't be like this," Autumn playfully pleaded with her friend.

"I have to dress up too! Ugh! There better be some fine-ass, rich men here, ma'am! I'm not playing with you, BIH!" Sasha continued.

"There will be rich men here, yes," Autumn said calmly.

.

"Damn it, Autumn!" Sasha said, annoyed. "You so lucky, I love you cause if I didn't, baby, I'd be out of here and leave yo ass stranded in New Orleans."

Autumn laughed quietly as she zipped up her burnt-orange velvet fitted dress. Sasha wore a similar dress, but it was chocolate in color. It was cold enough for booties, but still warm enough for a light jacket and scarf.

"Let's go to your nerdy thing and get dinner. You owe me huge and I'm going to collect," Sasha said.

Autumn laughed and said, "Deal!"

"The open house is going better than I expected," Mira said, pleased at the number of investors who had arrived and placed numerous offers. Bastion was doing a phenomenal job at presenting the newest technologies that would be installed and representing the companies.

Royce was, of course, charming all those who didn't speck technology and he gave a colorful and articulate history of the house quite eloquently. He discussed how the history would seamlessly intertwine with the modern-day amenities to give the end user a glimpse into the past as while moving into the future. "It's almost the end of the night, Mira. We should get dinner and drink to celebrate this family investment."

"And we shall. I'm just waiting on one more potential investor. She should be here any minute."

"Okay," Bastion said. "Will I need to give the entire spiel again or can I summarize?"

"Nah, she's pretty versed in the history of our house. She's looking to recreate a similar look for her future home."

"Oh, okay, then no need for me to hang around then," Bastion kissed his sister's cheek and turned to leave for his quarters.

"See you later for dinner then," Mira said, still watching the door.

"You know it," Bastion called down behind him.

As Bastion walked up the last steps to the second floor, he smelled honeysuckle and jasmine. He turned toward the heavy oak front doors and there stood Autumn. She and Sasha were the last visitors. *What the hell are they doing here?* Bastion said to himself, half excited and half curious.

He quickly and quietly moved back down the steps as Mira finished greeting the women. "Good evening, ladies! You look beautiful!"

"Girl, you too!" Sasha complimented Mira. "You are killing that Chanel and beat honey!"

Mira smiled and said, "Thanks, love! You ladies look just as spicy and delicious yourselves. Oh! This is my brother Sebastion. We own this house."

"I thought you left?" Mira whispered to him.

"I was going to. I thought I'd, you know, hang around and wait for you and Royce," he whispered back.

"Very nice to meet you, Mr. Robertson." Autumn felt her blood pressure rise as well as her temperature.

"Jones, could you take their jackets and scarves please?"

"Of course, Ms. Mira." Jones took the items and disappeared as quietly as he arrived.

"Bastion, this is Dr. Scorpeno and her best friend Sasha Mireno."

"Very nice to meet you also," Bastion said to Sasha.

"Likewise," Sasha said with a smirk on her face.

"Mira!" Royce yelled from the back room. "The last guests haven't arrived yet? Damn! I'm going to dinner without you bums!"

Mira was visibly annoyed by her brother but kept her cool and didn't reply. She spoke calmly and said, "Ladies, I do apologize for my brother's ignorance."

"No worries, Mira. It's all good," Autumn said genuinely, reassuring her. As Royce was walking into view from the back room, he recognized the last guests as the Nubian goddesses from the other night.

"Two nights in a row, huh? Are the gods really this generous? Oh yes! Thank you to all the gods," Royce said, just out of earshot.

Royce backed away and talked to Bastian through telepathy. 'B! Is that who I think it is?' Royce said like schoolboy.

Bastion, trying to control his face and smile, replied telepathically to his brother, 'Yeah!'

Royce cheered as if he'd just learned a huge secret.

'Bro, stop being weird and come out, just be cool and yourself,' Bastion thought.

'Bro! Sasha is fire!. Whew! Autumn's fine, too' Bastion nodded his head in agreement.

'Come on, bro!' Bastion encouraged Royce.

'On the way,' Royce said as he finally calmed down and relaxed.

"Hello, ladies, very nice to meet you," Royce said in the most charming voice.

"Ladies, this is Royce," Mira introduced him.

"Oooo," Sasha said in a sultry voice. "Hello Royce. Very nice to meet you."

"Likewise, darling," Royce replied, giving her bedroom eyes as he kissed the back of her hand and almost exposed his fangs.

"Well," Mira said. "Shall we proceed since introductions have been made?"

Yes, let's proceed," Autumn rushed, as she was feeling the heat from Bastion's gaze as she walked with Mira.

As they walked and talked, Sasha walked close to Autumn and whispered "Girl! Royce looks just as sexy as I hardly remember. Is that weird?" she worried.

Autumn laughed quietly as they walked through the hallways and looked into the various rooms. "I think I might like this white dude! OMG! Am I being weird? I am. Fuuuuck!" Sasha said with a little laughter.

Autumn kept laughing and then reassured her friend by giving her a big hug and said in her ear, "Do you, love. If that fine white man makes you feel some type of way then get after it."

Autumn was giving Sasha a dose of her own medicine. Sasha look at Autumn with a shocked look. "Really? Ms. I don't have time to date and have a regular life? Really? You think so?" Sasha seemed to be working up the nerve.

"Yeah girl! Do it!" Autumn said in her quietest Cardi B voice impression.

Sasha squealed and hugged Autumn then said, "Okay. I'm really about to holla at the fine-ass white dude. Only thing that would put him over the top would be if he had fangs."

Autumn laughed and said, "Bitch! You too nasty. " Sasha stuck out her tongue in agreement.

As they walked up to another room Sasha hugged her and whispered, "Maybe you'll work up the nerve to talk to Sabastion. Sober this time," She winked and walked just out of arm's reach. Autumn was appalled, but in a funny way. As they walked back toward the stairs to walk down, Royce appeared out of what seemed to be nowhere and offered to escort the ladies back down to the parlor area.

"Well, hello ladies," Royce smiled ever so charmingly. "I'd like to escort you back down to the parlor if you would allow me."

Sasha almost jumped over Autumn and said, "Why yes," in her sexiest voice. She wrapped her arm around his as Autumn took the other and they proceeded down.

While Sasha practically had a waterfall between her legs, Autumn laughed internally as they walked and talked with Royce. Autumn could see Sasha was really into him and smiled to herself and wished Royce all the luck with that wild one. As they entered the parlor, Mira was talking to another guest who had lingered behind. He was a very nice-looking Greek man who over stood more than six feet tall and looked extremely very fit.

"Hello, my dears. What do think? You see anything that sparked your intrigue or interest for inspiration in your home?"

Autumn was about to say yes, but Sasha blurted out, "Absolutely," as she eye fucked Royce.

Autumn cleared her throat as to draw attention back to the matter at hand. "Yes. Mira, this house is absolutely breathtaking," she said.

Mira smiled from ear to ear and said, "Fantastic! Does that mean you'll get in on the renovation of it?"

Autumn smiled and said confidently, "I'd love to."

"That's great news!" A rich, mahogany, baritone voice said from behind her. Autumn could feel her body temperature go up again as the voice and steps grew closer. *Goddamn, he smells so good*, she thought to herself as she snapped her eyes open before he could see they had closed.

"Indeed!" Mira said as she had moved closer to the gentleman she was talking to. She looked at him and he wrapped his arm around her waist. "Well ladies, if you would excuse us, we are going to say 'au revoir et bonne nuit' and then call it a night. Autumn, please give me a call tomorrow and we can discuss the details more." Mira's gentleman caller nodded toward them as he escorted Mira toward the doors.

"Awesome. Thank you so much, Mira. You're a fantastic host and I will." As Mira and her escort left the room, Sasha and Royce were causing the sexual tension in the room to heat up as he whispered to her and she giggled.

"Excuse me, Dr Scorpeno." Autumn could feel little sweat beads form on her back as she turned toward Sabastion.

"Good evening again, Mr. Robertson," she said, blushing. "It's very nice to … um … see you again." Autumn's peachy pink cheeks blushed harder and Bastion could see her pulse race and hear the blood rush through her veins.

"Likewise," Bastion felt bold and caved into his need to touch her, and gently grabbed her hand and brought it in for a gentle kiss. It was moist from the heat she was radiating and he loved it. She tasted heavenly. "

You look gorgeous," he said, finally coming up for air as he caught a wisp of her scent and she smelled of honeysuckle and jasmine.

"Thank you so much. You look delicious … oh my god … I mean dashing." Autumn's mind was moving faster than her mouth and she almost died of embarrassment on the spot.

Bastion smiled a sly grin and said a little closer to her, "It's okay. So do you." He winked.

Sensing that she still felt nervous and embarrassed, he suggested a change of atmosphere. "Would you like to see the balcony to get some fresh air?" He offered her his arm.

Autumn looked for Sasha who was tongue deep into Royce's face and said, "Yeah, seems they need some privacy too."

Bastion looked over and quietly laughed. "Indeed."

As the two made their way to the balcony, unbeknownst to Bastion, they were being watched. Cathrine Ortega of the Barcelonina Clan was not one to be rejected, nor was she one to take no for an answer. She had been with Sabastion 100 years ago and was still determined to have him all to herself. Cathrine drove a high-end Maserati and had just pulled up to the house. As she parked her car directly in front of the house, the valet came running out to assist. "You scratch it, I'll eat you. Comprende? She said to the scared valet. "Si, Senora Ortega," he answered as he picked up the keys She had dropped them on the ground, as she always did, rather than hand anything to anyone.

"Where's Jones? Jones!" The man in question came out to the foyer as Senora Ortega walked in.

"Si Senora?"

"Where's Mira? We need to talk."

Jones, not scared of anyone or thing, answered nonchalantly, "She's with her gentleman for the rest of the evening, Senora. Shall I tell her you've an urgent matter to talk to her about? Yes, Jones. Damn," Catherine said in an annoyed voice.

"Very well, Senora. Please have a seat in the living room."

As Jones dashed off to notify Mira, Cathrine walked around the living room, seething.

"Hey Cat. What's up?" Mira was in her bathrobe and looked annoyed as she came into the living room.

"Who is that with Sabastion?" Cat wanted to know immediately.

"She's a mortal doctor named Autumn Scorpeno. Why?"

"What is she doing here? Cathrine starting to interrogate Mira.

"Girl, first of all," Mira started, getting more annoyed with Cat. "She's an investor for the project and none of your business."

"Damn…okay!" Cat responded, trying not to upset Mira anymore, since Mira was Cathrine's unknowing source for inside information about Bastion.

"I'm just wondering why a doctor would want to invest in renovation properties here, especially this house."

"Look, Cat, I don't care why she's interested, her money spends just like ours does and I'm not about to waste it."

Cathrine heard Mira, but she couldn't get the thought of Bastion preferring a mortal over her out of her head. *She is in the way of me getting Bastion back.*

Mira snapped her fingers in front of Cathrine's snarling face. "Earth to Cathrine. What's wrong with you?"

"Nothing!" Cathrine replied. "I was just wondering about that and how Bastion was doing, you know being back here and all."

Mira gave her a side eye and said, "Um hum. He's fine and minding his business. Like you should be."

Cat turned toward Mira and reached out for a hug. Mira raised an eyebrow, but leaned in. They hugged and finally Cat said, "Honestly Mira, I don't care if Bastion is seeing her. We were 100 years ago, so it's all good."

Mira side eyed her again and said, "Girl, have a drink or three and go get laid. You're stressed and pressed for no reason." Mira walked back toward the stairs to her bed while Cathrine stayed behind to ponder her next move.

"I don't know what you want from her, Sabastion, but she's not good enough for you. I'll make sure you see know that." Cathrine smiled a horribly deviant smile, as she was devising an evil scheme. As she finally found some kind of peace in her crazed state of mind, she walked outside of the house and zeroed in on the balcony. She watched, seething, as Autumn and Bastion laughed and talked. Their conversation was just out of earshot, but she could tell he was intrigued with the mortal. She snarled as her fangs descended. *Bitch, your time is coming*, Cathrine thought.

Soon her Maserati was pulled up to her as pristine as it was when she dropped it off. She snatched the keys from the valet, looked back at the balcony once more, then got into the car and sped off. As the house became smaller in her rearview mirror she said in a black-eyed, fanged, voice of rage, "Soon, Sabastion. You'll be mine again and this time forever."

*   *   *

"So what brings you to the estate? You plan to invest as my sister hopes or just looking for home-decor inspiration?" Bastion asked.

Autumn still shook from seeing him up close and personal again, looking like a whole snack. "Um, yes. That's kind of the plan."

Bastion laughed and said, "Yes to both then?"

Autumn realized she hadn't really given an answer. "Apologies for being rude. It was kind of warm in there," she said, finally coming back to her senses.

Bastion laughed a deep, primal sound as he crept a little closer to her. Autumn, not noticing him moving closer, finally said, "So you're a Robertson? Like the oldest English-Scot clan Robertsons?"

"Yes," Bastion smiled.

Ugh that smile is dangerous … focus, Autumn, she reminded herself. "Wow, so you're old money rich. Like rich rich." Bastion burst out laughing. *OMG, he's so gorgeous and he smells just as blessed,* Autumn thought as he kept smiling at her question.

Bastion thought her naivete and innocence were beautiful. He finally said with a smile, "I guess you could say that."

Autumn continued, "But you only own that little gem of a bookstore?"

Bastion was at ease.

He would answer any and all questions she had about him because he felt something was different about her. She was different from the others. He felt something he'd never felt before. "Yes, it's all mine." He smiled now, closer to her so he was continually in the flow of her essence. She smelled so delicious.

"But you are super wealthy? I mean, I guess you can do whatever with your money, but I don't know. I mean …" Autumn laughed at herself because she couldn't quite put words and sentences together, as he seemed to be getting closer into her personal space. She was sweating again, even though the crisp fall breeze was gently blowing through the trees.

Bastion smiled slightly. "Does it bother you that I'm not as flashy as most wealthy people?"

"No!" Autumn corrected herself quickly. "No, not at all. I mean I don't know." Autumn was now at a loss for words as the air smelled like mahogany and teakwood. The air around them was thick with his scent and she was intoxicated.

Autumn took a deep breath in and decided to speak her mind. "Honestly, I thought you were this really …" Autumn began to bite her lip, making him semi hard. "This really cute, nerdy guy who owned the bookstore and had a simple one- or two-bedroom apartment close by. You know, nothing fancy, but not a typical bachelor pad. Something vintage and rich, with warm colors if that doesn't sound weird." Autumn was blushing again as she tried to hide her smile from him. He had such piercing eyes and they were too much to look into deeply without being hypnotized. Bastion laughed that sexy sound again. *Calm down Autumn*, she reminded herself.

"Aren't you intuitive?" He smiled, now close enough she could practically feel the heat radiating from him. "That's exactly how I live. I have an apartment over the bookstore. It's a cozy two bedroom."

As she finally looked up to him, his eyes were icy blue in the moonlight. Autumn felt entranced. "So you live simply? Why? You don't like lavish things?" The questions came automatically, as she became more hypnotized by his allure and the way he stared into her soul. She was feeling breathless and spoke softer, as he was closer now. He placed his hand on hers while slightly leaning in toward her.

"Autumn, living lavishly is all in the mindset of the person," he began. "I'm happy with my simple life," he said with a slight smile, as he could hear her heart beat racing, almost a sweet, humming sound. "I invest my money and am very well to do, but not every jewel and precious metal is material." He finally worked up the nerve to grab her waist and pull her closer. As he did, Autumn felt her heart skip a beat and stop. Her body felt as though it was on fire, and he could see the sweat droplets form on her skin.

She stared at him with those illuminated golden eyes as if they burned with hot lava. "Autumn, do you remember what you whispered to me the other night?"

Autumn stiffened and said "Um, Bastion, I'm normally not that type of girl to just, umm, you know, give it up and I … *So wet. Really want to kiss his mouth. OMG, are those fangs?. Am I dripping?*

"Autumn…," Bastion whispered practically into her mouth as he said, "talk to me." And proceeded to kiss her.

"Ugh…," Autumn's moan almost sent him into a sex-driven rage. He was dangerously close to snatching her dress and panties off. He gently slid his hand between and up her slick, golden thighs. To his delight, he found she wasn't wearing any panties.

Bastion, now fully erect loudly whispered, "OMG, Autumn." Bastion could barely breathe as he felt the droplets of sweet nectar drip from her hidden lotus flower.

He imagined her pussy tasting as sweet as her lips. She welcomed his tongue as she took more of his scent and fingers into her. Bastion curled and uncurled his fingers inside her as if he was calling her to cum.

"Oooooh, Bastion," she moaned breathlessly. "Oh my, ugh! Autumn was soggy and could feel the juices running down her legs, but she didn't care at this moment.

"Yes, my gorgeous Nubian queen. Cum for me, my beautiful unicorn," Bastion said, continuing to penetrate her garden ever so gently and deeply kiss her.

As his fingers sunk deeper into her secret stash of golden honey, she gasped, "I'm going to cum. Ugh." Bastion held her close and began to finger her harder and faster. "OMG, Bastion! Yes!" She would have screamed if he hadn't covered her mouth with his own. His fangs were fully extended now and as she began to climax she cut her tongue on his fang and bled into his mouth.

OMG, She's fucking magical! Bastions eyes popped wide open and were almost a light gray color.

Bastion practically came in his pants.

"I'm cumming!!! she moaned into his mouth. It was mind blowing. Bastion's eyes were fully light gray and full of electricity. His fangs were dripping blood from Autumn's mouth, but right now Autumn couldn't wrap her mind around what had just happened. "Bastion" she finally moaned, coming down from the stratosphereic orgasm she'd just experienced. "Bastion … you're … um … I mean … um."

Bastion smiled as he held her close to him. He gently kissed and hugged her, keeping himself submerged in her sweet scent. "Autumn, you're an incredible woman and I want you to myself."

Autumn, looking half excited and half skeptical, said, "Bastion, you are an amazing man, but let's be real for a moment. You come from an extremely rich and very white bloodline and I'm not sure if this … us … would be accepted, especially on your side. You know what I mean?" Bastion, looking more serious now, understood and respected her viewpoint.

"Autumn, it's 2021. So much has happened in this day and age and, honestly, if people can't see past skin color by now they aren't worth yours or my time. Just give me a chance," Bastion almost pleaded.

She turned away from him to face the night sky as he held her from behind. "I don't know, Bastion." In her head, she was debating herself, *Girl, no! This was fun and shit, but do you really want extra problems? Girl! This man is fine and is everything you said you've wanted and then some in a lover, companion, and oh, shit, … life partner. Just give him a chance, Bitch! What could it hurt?*

"Autumn, where'd you go?" Bastion whispered, interrupting her internal debate. Bastion watched as he could practically see the wheels in her beautiful mind turn. He finally turned her to face him. Against the starry night sky and the smell of honeysuckle and jasmine, he was intoxicated. "Autumn, my beautiful Nubian goddess." Bastion wrapped his muscular arms around her waist, resting them on her voluptuous hips. He bit his lip in a sly smile, looking into those golden jewel eyes. "Give me thirty days to prove to you that you are for me and only me. If I can't prove it to you then you'll never see me again."

Autumn looked deeply into his now-ocean-blue eyes and continued to inhale his scent. *Damn it he smells so good. UGH! Okay bitch what are we going to do?* The voices in her head yelled. Bastion looked nervous as she went quiet on him again. "Love? Autumn, honey, say something."

"Yes," she finally got the nerve and courage to say.

Bastion looked shocked. "Yes as in you'll give me thirty days?" he confirmed.

Autumn blushed and smiled. "Yes, I'll give you thirty days, Mr. Robertson," she winked.

Yeesss! Bastion pulled her closer and pressed a smiling kiss down on her face.

She smiled at his enthusiasm and said, "Yes, love. But the time will start when I get back to Saint Louis. Deal?"

"Yes, my love. Deal!" Bastion kept kissing her.

"Ohh. This weekend, sir," she said more confidently and assertively "Was a trial run." She winked.

OMG…she's so firey and I fucking love it! "Yes, ma'am," Bastion finally replied, grinning.

"Autumn!" Sasha called from the downstairs foyer. "Our Uber's here!"

Autumn looking slightly disappointed, but still very satisfied. "Well, Mr. Sneaky Bookstore owner, I guess I'll be seeing you soon then." Autumn got up on her tiptoes and kissed his lips. "Fuck!" she mouthed as she came back down with a smile.

"Autumn! Let's go!" Sasha called again.

"I'm coming! Damn, hold on!" As she ran down the stairs, Autumn looked back at Bastion and waved goodbye. He waved back, holding his member down, and thought *I'll win you over Autumn my queen. You'll see. I'll show you I'm everything you need me to be.*

"What's up, B? What's good?" Royce asked, coming out of nowhere as the girls rode off in their luxury Uber. Bastion kept looking in the direction of his future, not saying anything. "Damn, bro, you look like you had a very good conversation with the good doctor," Royce teased. "Was it good"? He was being curious now. .

Bastion tasted his fingers, thought about how delicious her pussy and blood tasted, and simply said, "It was the fucking best I've ever had."

"You let him do what?" Sasha squealed and acted like she couldn't hear Autumn's answer. She asked multiple questions on the way back to the hotel.

"Shut up!" Autumn blushed as she told her best friend what a beautifully sexy evening she had.

"So, you gave him thirty days to show you that you're his long-lost love or some shit like that. OMG!" Sasha laughed.

Autumn smiled and ignored Sasha's skepticism. "See, this is why I don't tell you shit!" Autumn said in a pouty kind of way.

"No, No, Okay for real," Sasha finally composed herself. "So his fangs and eyes are real for real? Like really real?"

"Yeah, I think so."

Sasha was wide eyed and speechless till they got into their room. "BIH, that explains so much about his brother!" Sasha said.

"What do you mean?" Autumn looked back as she was getting out of her dress for a shower before getting into bed.

"Girl! When I was chatting Royce up, he kept licking his mouth."

Autumn gave her a playful side eye. "Really, your thotiness?" she laughed.

"Shut up!" Sasha laughed. "I kept it real classy and chill, you know me," she winked. Autumn laughed as Sasha continued. "He said, 'What did I do to deserve the pleasure of seeing you twice?' I gave him the sly smile and said 'Maybe it's just your lucky weekend.'" Autumn laughed as Sasha demonstrated how she had played coy. "He did give me a kind of fangy smile, but I thought I was seeing what I wanted to see, you know what I mean?." Sasha winked and stuck out her tongue. . "Anyway, we talked more and drank a lot more and he asked me if I tasted as delicious as I smelled. So, you know me bitch. In my mind I was like 'Hell, yeah, bitch! It's going down!' I smiled at him and finally said, 'You trying to find out?' Then it happened!"

"BIH! What?" Autumn screamed as she fell over on her bed.

"I know, right?" Sasha screamed back. "Bitch, his eyes went from a light brown to a super peridot green and he has real fangs! I'm talking real real fangs! Bitch, I almost came right then."

Autumn screamed again with excitement. "BIH, then what?" She was here for all the tea.

Sasha smiled that as-a-matter-of-fact smile and said, "This dude ate my pussy like shark week. I ain't never came so damn hard and much in my life," Sasha said, out of breath fro, reliving the moment.

"Girl! I might love this white-ass vampire. Shit!" Sasha laughed.

Autumn's mouth hung open and then finally they both screamed with excitement again. "This was the best weekend ever!" Sasha hugged Autumn tight.

"Thank you, love, for everything," Sasha finally said as she pulled away from Autumn. "Now get your light ass in the shower and get some sleep. Tomorrow we fly back to reality. Let's see what the next thirty days holds."

Sasha finally left her room and Autumn was left with her thoughts of Bastion. She finally showered and got cozy in bed, and then her phone dinged. Saint Louis area code … okay. The text read "Autumn, this is Sabastion. I know the thirty days doesn't start till you get back, but I wanted to tell you thirty days is only the beginning. I want you forever and am going to prove it to you. Also, your book arrived Call you soon. Yours, Bastion." A wink emoji was after the sentence about her book. Autumn squealed and blushed as she re-read the message before closing her eyes. *Thirty days is only the beginning…we'll see.* Autumn drifted off to sleep in hope that her dreams led her back to Bastion.

"Good morning, little bro! Let's get some breakfast! Get your dick out of the mattress and let's go!" Royce yelled and laughed through FaceTime. Bastion looked at the screen with one eye, trying to focus, gave his brother the middle finger, and then hung up. Bastion rolled over on his back, finally awake, and thought for a few minutes. *That dream felt so real.* Bastion lay there, trying to recapture the sounds, smells, and tastes from the night. He slid his hand down his abs to the top of his boxer briefs and gripped himself as if his hand was Autumn's pussy. Bastion closed his eyes and relived the dream. *Autumn. my beautiful Nubian goddess … come to me, lass.* Bastion watched as Autumn walked slowly in. She wore red-bottomed heels with the robe of thinnest silk he had made just for her. Her hair was down and in a beautiful golden crown of curls. Her curvaceous body moved smoothly under the robe.

It was just short enough to see the very top of her thighs and, as she turned to model it for him, her perfect peach peaked out from under it like it was teasing him to take a bite out of it. His eyes began to change to the icy blue as he became aroused. He let out a primal growl as her presence made him feel alive and precum began to flow. "Touch me, my love. Feel what you have awakened." Her hand extended toward him and he grabbed it and pulled her into him.

Autumn was breathing heavily and said Bastion "Lover, your … um … size is … I'm a little nervous."

Bastion smiled into her neck and curls and reassured her, whispering,

"My beautiful, angelic creature, my love. I promise to be as gentle as I can with you."

Autumn's eyes seemed to glow a shimmery, liquid-gold color as she stared into his eyes. "Goddamn, you're beautiful."

She turned her eyes down as she blushed and caught a glimpse of him, her mouth beginning to water.

"Lass, tell me what you want. Tell me your deepest desires, my queen, and I'll give them to you."

Autumn was suddenly filled with an urge. He felt her body heat up and she whispered, "I want to taste you."

Bastion almost fainted as his little golden unicorn goddess said these words. "Are you sure?" he said, short of breath. He didn't want to push her or make her feel uncomfortable, but hoped he had heard her correctly.

She gripped him through his silk pajama pants and pulled him out. Bastion let his head fall back, was helpless under her touch. "Bastion," she said in a sultry tone. "You smell so good my love."

"Oh, yes," he growled.

"Wait, my love, let's get more comfortable first."

Bastion took a few deep breathes to do as she instructed. They moved over to his California king-sized bed. "Stand here, lover."

"Yes, my goddess," Bastion said breathless and obediently. She stroked him gently with one hand and untied his pants with the other. As she slid his pants down over his hips, her eyes widened and her mouth and pussy started to drip with excitement, awaiting this moment. She was in awe at his fully erect ten inches of glory. "Are you still nervous, my love?" Bastion stood tall and stared deep into Autumn's glowing, hypnotic eyes. Autumn looked down at the prize, then looked back up at him with the naughtiest of smiles and gave his member the gentlest of swipes with her tongue. Bastion thought he was going to bust right there, but held it together. He growled louder and deeper now. It sounded like a mating call of big cats in wild. "Autumn, my goddess, don't tease me, lass." Autumn smirked at him, opened her tiny mouth, and began to slowly descend down his shaft. "Oh my god!" he growled. Autumn's mouth was so wet and warm. He was getting high from the sensation. She inhaled him and created a vacuum-like fit around his member.

As she took him into her mouth, it seemed like her throat went on forever. Bastion practically melted as Autumn sucked and swirled her tongue around his dick. She could feel her juices dripping down her thighs as she pleasured herself. "Love," Bastion struggled to say. "I'm going to cum, lass!"

Autumn, now fully into her tantric state, whispered to him, "Do it, baby."

Bastion's eyes slid shut and Autumn's rhythm picked up she sucked harder. "Uggghh … Autumn!" he roared. Bastion's deep voice screamed her name as he let go. Autumn drank all of him as he fell to the bed. Not losing a single drop of him, she licked her lips and the corners of her mouth.

"Autumn, love. You … you are a goddess," Bastion said, trying to catch his breath.

Autumn smiled as she kissed up his torso. "You look satisfied, love," she said with a dangerously sweet, sexy smile.

Her voice was like a siren's song, sweet, seductive, and deadly. He loved it. With that life draining orgasm and the re-energizing of Bastion's life energy, he was ready to return all the favors. He flipped Autumn over on her back faster then she could imagine. He positioned himself between her almond-colored thick and juicy thighs. He could feel the heat coming from her pussy as the scent of honeysuckle tickled his nose. Autumn's breath became shallow as Bastion kissed down her stomach. "Your body is a beautiful temple, goddess. I want to worship you forever." As he kissed down her body, he made sure to caress every tattoo on her body. One tattoo of a phoenix intrigued him. He kissed her thighs, then the top of her pussy and Autumn held her breath. "Relax, goddess, I'll be gentle. I promise."

He smiled into her skin as she slowly relaxed and he began to work his magic. As she breathed a slight sigh of relief, he took that opportunity to slip his fingers into her waiting wet pussy. "Oooohh, Bastion, don't stop," she moaned as he stroked her clit to make her pussy drip its sweet, sticky nectar. In and out, round and round his fingers twisted inside her. Her body began to contort and bend as though he was conjuring up her sex demons.

"Goddess, I want to worship you. You aren't of this world!"

"Bastion!" she said breathlessly. "I'm going to cum! Ugh!" She was ascending to her climax.

"Not yet, my love! I want to taste you first." He slowed his pace. "I want to taste your wild nectar and drink of your galaxy." Bastion spread her thighs and, with his fangs fully extended, began to drink and devour her.

He gently slid his tongue into her throbbing wetness and she screamed, "Bastion! Ohhhh!"

"Relax, love. I promised to be gentle." As he drank deeply and more aggressively, she felt her oceans run down. "Oh my god, Autumn, you taste magical my love." He bit the inside of her thigh, causing her to jump and her gush extra hard. She arched her back even further as he gripped her peachy ass to better access her sweet, tender flesh.

He could see her eye flicker from gold to silver and her body radiated heat. Bastion loved it. "Goddess, you taste so … mmmm. You taste of the forbidden fruit," He growled into her pussy.

"Ugh…yesss! Bastion! Don't stop!"

She was moments from glory when Bastion said, "Don't cum yet gorgeous."

"Ugh, I can't hold it!" she struggled to say.

Bastion quickly rose to reposition himself at the opening of her garden. "Hold on, goddess, I want you to experience what immortality has to offer." Autumn vaguely heard what he said. She was too high in the stratosphere and wasn't coming down. Then she realized as he eased himself inside her.

"Be gentle, Bastion," she whispered as she braced herself.

"As much as I can, my love," he said, almost losing control. As he began to inch deeper into her he almost erupted. "Ugh! Goddess, you are so tight."

"Oh, my god! Yes!" Autumn gripped him as she arched her back to open up. "Gentle," she could barely get out. Bastion was struggling also.

He began to sweat as the need to plunge into her fully built up within him. Inching slowly deeper into her was becoming too much for him. "Autumn, I need to fill you!" Bastion groaned. Her eyes shot open, as she wasn't ready. Before she could get the words out, though, he growled loud and plunged deep into her. She screamed, torn between pain and pleasure. She was soaking wet, and felt him in what seemed like her stomach.

Him that deep inside her tight sheath caused her body to ignite. The tightness and pulsing of his dick inside her eased the pressure. Her body was so hot.

Bastion nervously asked, "Are you okay?" He would have been devastated if he had ruined this beautiful moment for them. Autumn's eyes, now a liquid-mercury silver, stared into his worried sweaty face.

"Shhhhh," she said. "Please me, Sabastion."

With that reassurance, he began to rock back and forth inside her sheath, deeper and deeper as they climbed toward the stratosphere. Bastion's fangs ached to sink his teeth into her. "Goddess! Oh, my god!" Bastion growls grew louder and louder and Autumn's moans were just as beautiful as her naked wet skin against his. The deeper and harder he thrust, the louder they both became. Her skin heated up hotter and started to change color, radiating a golden-red hue. Her tattoos began to change into reds, oranges, and gold feather shapes and her fingernails seemed to turn to talons.

"Yes! Bastion! Harder!" Bastion was sweating profusely, but was in a trance. "I'm going to cum!" Autumn screamed. Her gold hair had turned to golden strands of fire.

"Me too, my love!" Autumn reached up around his neck and dug her newly formed talons into his back. Bastion arched his back, and her obvious pleasure sent him into his primal state. His fangs fully descended, eyes icy blue, he grabbed her hips and slammed into her.

"Oh! Oh! Oh!" She screamed.

"Come for me, goddess!" Bastion roared as he slammed into her again and again. Her scream sounded like the call of the phoenix and, as she released it, he bit down on her neck.

The rush of hot, sticky- sweet blood filled his mouth and turned his eyes light gray. He drank deeply of her blood as she screeched, "I'm coming!"

Autumn's body was literally on fire, but Bastion wasn't burned. As Bastion drank of her spicy-sweet blood, he growled loudly and erupted inside of her. He fell into a cosmic trance as they rode the galactic waves of the own private universe.

"Goddess," Bastion finally said as he rolled onto his back. They were both out of breath and energy. "I want to worship you forever."

Autumn's body was finally cooling down and returning to its natural golden-brown hue. Her skin still glowed against the candlelight and the dampness from their mystical experience.

"Autumn," Bastion said as he looked down to find his beauty fast asleep, cuddled into him. He kissed her warm head of wet curls "Forever, my goddess. You are mine."

"Bastion! Boy, stop beating off and let's go!" Royce yelled as he burst into his room.

Bastion sat up in his bed and said, "Royce, Autumn's a phoenix."

"What?" Royce said, from Bastion's closet where he was trying on Bastion's jackets.

"Bro! Get out of my shit!" Bastion yelled as he got up out of his bed. "Listen, Autumn is a mystical creature. She's a fucking phoenix!"

Royce finally stepped out of Bastion's closet, wearing his new Givenchy jacket. " Bro, I don't know what you drank or smoked, but I want some. You know that species of the lore died out eons ago. They were gone way before the first vampires appeared." Royce looked at the disheveled bed and side eyed Bastion as he said, "You nasty."

"Whatever, bitch," Bastion said from his bathroom. He took a quick shower and shaved, then pulled his pants on and finally opened the door. " I know the legend of the phoenix, but what if they just evolved to survive? Like evolved so much that they intertwined their genes into mortals to stay safe from extinction."

Royce saw his brother really thinking hard about this. "Yeah, that'd be dope if it turns out to be true. A phoenix, huh? How do you know or think you know?" Royce seemed intrigued also.

Bastion leaned in toward his brother as if to tell him the secret. "It's none of your fucking business!" Bastion yelled in his face. Royce reached out to punch and push his brother, but he was too slow to make contact. "Now get out so I can finish getting dressed."

Royce, looking perturbed, said, "Fine! Don't tell me, dick!"

As Royce turned to the door, Bastion said "Hey! Leave my jacket, bitch."

"Ugh! Damn, you stingy."

Bastion laughed as Royce threw the jacket. When his brother closed the door, he sat down in his large lounge chair and pondered his new revelation about Autumn. "I'm in love with a phoenix goddess." He smiled as he thought about how lucky he was and how the universe seemed to be smiling down on him.

*　*　*

"Damn, it's so good to be home," Autumn said as she crossed her threshold and dropped her bags. She breathed a sigh of relief as she took off her shoes and plopped down on her couch. She lived in a spacious three-bedroom, two-bath condo that was quite cozy. It was filled with flowers of all kinds, colors, and books. She had colorful mandala patterns and star formations. Her favorite place in the whole house was her bedroom. In her room, she had designed a ceiling light that dimmed. At its lowest setting, it twinkled like the stars.

As she ran her bathwater, she turned on her favorite Sade playlist and dimmed the lights to twinkle. It was the small pleasures in life that made her evening. After long fourteen to sixteen hour days, she found peace in her wine and king-sized bed after a hot bath. As she slid into the tub, she grabbed her phone and re-read the message from Sabastion. "Thirty days is only the beginning." Autumn let her mind sail away with the sounds of her music, the candlelight, and stars. As she stepped out of the tub, she caught a glimpse of herself. She stood a stacked five foot six inches with a twenty-nine inch waist and a peach for an ass. She also had tattoos. Lots of them. Her favorite, though, was her phoenix. It was the biggest piece she had, and it covered her entire left side. It was fire red, orange, and gold. It kind of called to her when she decided to get it. She felt more complete and whole once she got it, like it was a missing piece of her family and now it was home. As she rubbed the cocoa butter over her skin, she imagined her hands were Sabastion's instead. She rubbed the butter up her legs and thighs and rubbed her fingers against pussy. She let out a sigh and brought herself back. *Damn it! What's wrong with you? Bitch, get it together! You had a great weekend, damn it! Now it's back to reality. If seeing you was a priority, then he would have already made some kind of move. UGH! Relax and see what happens.*

As she was finally relaxed and refreshed with her plushy robe on, her intercom rang. She got up off the couch and ran over to the intercom. "Yes?"

"Delivery for Dr. Scorpeno!"

"I'm coming!" She ran down the hall and rode the elevator down to the lobby.

"Delivery, Ms. Sign here, please. Thank you," The courier said as he gave her an extremely decorative box.

"Oooo! I didn't order anything this fancy."

Back in her condo, she sat cross legged on her bed and opened the attached card. *Autumn, this is an invitation to the new planetary observatory ... in Switzerland. I'd love for you to join me this week for a private viewing of the world's most powerful telescope in the world. In this box, you'll find a small token of my gratitude for your company. Yours, Sabastion. P.S. I want to give you the stars. This way you can you pick the one you want the most.* A wink emoji ended the message.

She smelled the card and squealed a little. It smelled like him. She opened the box and unfolded the red paper. It was the most beautiful sequined dress. The tag said Vera Wang Private Collection. "Oh my god!" she squealed. "It's stunning!" Inside the big box were smaller boxes. The shoebox had Louboutin Red Bottoms that she thought were supposed to be released next winter. The smallest box held a diamond-studded choker necklace and a bracelet. Autumn sat in awe of what Sabastion had sent. "Well, shit…," she said with a cheesy grin. In the card was another envelope. "Ooo, what's this?" They were first class plane tickets on Emirates Airlines. Her mouth fell open as she read that and she screamed into her pillow with excitement.

She grabbed her phone and Facetimed Sasha.

"What's up, boo?" Sasha said casually.

"Bitch! Guess what I got?"

Sasha stopped typing to pay attention. "What, bitch?" she said.

"I'll show you!" Autumn said proudly. She walked Sasha through all the gifts.

Sasha squealed, "Yes, babe! So you're going to do nerdy stuff in Switzerland? Bitch! I love it!"

Autumn laughed and gave her the finger! "I'm just saying, I think you should go and do all the nasty, vampire-fanged things!"

Autumn laughed and said confidently, I'm going to go and I may do some—some!—nasty things." She winked.

Sasha's eyes got big and she screamed with excitement. "Okay, Bitch I gotta go, but hit me up later so we can pack your shit for this nerdy, nasty trip. Handcuffs and frames." Sasha stuck out her tongue and hung up.

Autumn smelled the card again and fell to the bed. She was falling … for Sabastion.

*   *   *

Sebastion's phone pinged. He was currently in a meeting with the Spanish Vampire clans and his sister Mira. "Greetings, Ortega Family! We have an opportunity to expand our companies to the far ends of the earth. This can happen with the new technologies Sebastion's company is developing. Bastion, could you give them some background on it?"

"Of course." As Sebastion readied himself, Catherine couldn't take her eyes off of him. She was the sister of the head of the Ortega Clan. She got whatever and whoever she wanted. "Ladies and Gentlemen, my companies are developing the newest and latest in vampire sun protection. For too long we have skated the lines of death every day to live among the mortals as normally as possible. We have made advanced strides for sun protection for homes and vehicles, but now, ladies and gentlemen, we've made a breakthrough medically. No more harmful sunscreens that burn the skin, cause discoloration, or, worse yet, poison us making us vulnerable.

"With this new skin graft, it is possible to finally live fully in the sun. Once implanted, the grafted skin adapts to the existing skin and grows rapidly over the epidermis, providing overall protection. This new skin adapts so much it tans and lightens as the seasons change, and it pulls and flexes just as normal skin does. Best of all, it is made specifically for vampires. We will be able to blend in and mingle, meaning more opportunities for us as a species. We currently have test subjects in Hawaii, Alaska, Miami, and Dubai. They are reporting phenomenal results, and if that continues we'll be ready for mass production within the year.

"Vampires can finally live among the rest of the Lore without worrying about dying," he continued. "Best of all, no more living in the shadows." The room was quiet when he finished. Sebastion could feel the tension in the room.

"Thank you, Sebastion." The head of the Ortega clan finally said after reading some of the data from the reports. Mr. Zepher was the patriarch of the family. "Living as mortals, huh? That's beneath me and all vampires."

"Mr. Ortega, living shouldn't have to be done only at night," Sebastion replied. "It's 2021 and vampires are still living in the shadows. The faires, lycans, witches, and so on of the lore are finding new ways to live peacefully and safely among the mortals. They live undetected and un afraid of being hunted or killed." Mr. Zepher listened to Sebastion's speech for peace and rolled his eyes. " You know, Sebastion, in 21 your parents and my wife Luisa and I lived peacefully without the mortal trash. I've heard enough. I'm ready to leave." Mr. Zepher got up, as did the others at the table.

"Mr. Zepher, if you'd just hear me out…," Sebastion tried to continue.

Mira first spotted Mr. Zepher's annoyance with her brother's persistence. "Brother." She grabbed his arm. "It's all good. Let's just go."

"James will see you to the lobby. Live like mortals … phssst." Mr. Zepher walked slowly out of the room with his cronies in tow.

Catherine, however, ran to catch up with Sebastion and Mira, and looped her arm in with Bastion's. "Don't worry, love, I'll talk to him. He'll come around."

Bastion pulled away and politely said, "Thanks, Catherine, but I'll take my company's business elsewhere. It's all good."

Catherine wasn't too thrilled about being curved, but she wasn't about to give up. As she walked with them to the Range Rover, she asked Bastion, "Do you have plans this week? Maybe you'd like to join me on the new hundred-foot yacht. Zepher got it for me for my millenium birthday. We can … umm … you know, christen it a few times at sea and wake up to our own waves." She paused, waiting for his response. "Sebastion! Are you listening?"

"What? Sorry Catherine, I didn't catch that."

She was pissed. "Did you hear anything I said? What is up with you, Sebastion?" she asked, annoyed.

"Nothing is up. You need to chill out. What did you say?" Sebastion asked.

"I wanted to know if you wanted to fuck on my new boat for the week," she said in her sexiest voice.Catherine had legs that went on for days. She modeled for the most famous magazines around the world. She was as pale and perfect as they come, and they certainly did. She could have almost anything or anyone she wanted … almost. Bastion was a fish outside of her ocean of choices and she wanted him. Badly.

"Nah, I'm good, love," Sebastion said nonchalantly. "I have plans already."

Cat's mouth flew open, as being rejected wasn't something she was used to.

"Why not?" she asked, standing between him and the door to his car.

Bastion looked visibly annoyed. "Girl, I told you, I'm good and I have plans. Excuse me." He gently moved her aside and got into the car. As he pulled away she yelled, "You got plans with that black mortal I saw you with the other night?"

Bastion slammed on the brakes and backed up to where she was standing. He got out of the car, black eyes hard as stone as he towered over her smaller frame. "First of all, Catherine, you're a real bitch, you know that? You're a spoiled-ass brat. Second, her name is Dr. Autumn Scorpeno and, yes, I have plans with her. Lastly, it's absolutely none of your fucking business." Calmly he added, "Now, if you'll excuse me. Being nice to you has drained the positive energy out of me. Adios."

Catherine was extremely pissed, but aroused. "What's so special about a mortal when you can have me?"

He turned around as he was getting back into the car and said, "I'd rather not be a pet to a bitch," and drove off. As he pulled away he could see her standing there, her mouth hanging wide open, fuming.

Mira, who had watched it unfold said in disbelief, "Well, Autumn must be something very special, little bro. Can't wait to hear the story." Mira winked and squeezed her brother's arm.

Bastion smiled. *She is indeed very special.*

Catherine, still seething from her encounter with Bastion, was more determined than ever. If I can't have you, Sebastion Roberston, I'll make damn sure you can't have precious doctor mortal bitch." Catherine scratched her claws against the building, making deep marks in the stone.

*   *   *

Walking into his apartment, all Sebastion could think of was Autumn. *Did she receive my gift? What did she think? Did it make her smile?* Those questions and more ran through his head as he undressed from the disaster of a meeting with the Ortega Family. When he finally sat back down on his bed after grabbing a pair of basketball shorts, he grabbed his phone and saw a message from Autumn. He felt the heat and excitement from what she could have said in her message.

All the message read was "Yes!" with excited and heart-eyed emojis. Bastion smiled at his phone, as he knew this was just the beginning. He jumped up with new energy in his step as he Googled flower shops. He called the flower shop closest to the bookstore that had rapid delivery. He considered what flowers he wanted to send her, but he couldn't think straight due to his thoughts of the future. He FaceTimed Jones. *He would know.*

"Good evening, Sir. How may I be of service?"

"Hey Jones, can you tell me what kind of flowers say 'I can't wait to see you and be ready for a fantastic week'?"

Jones thought for a moment. "Sir, how about some white lilies, purple orchids, and yellow roses."

"Nice!" Bastion said taking notes. "Thanks Jones. You're the best."

"Anytime, sir," Jones said, hanging up.

Bastion called the flower shop and gave the order. The florist was surprised at how specific and large the order was. Bastion had bought the store's entire stock of yellow roses, white lilies, and purple orchids. "Is this everything sir?"

Bastion imagined how Autumn would react around when she received the flowers.

"Yes," he beamed. "What you like the card to say?" The florist was impressed at the effort this man was putting in.

Bastion thought about it for a moment and smirked. Please write, "See you soon, with a wink emoji."

"Right away, sir."

"Thank you so much." Bastion gave the florist the address of the hospital where Autumn worked.

"They will be delivered today."

"Thank you again," Bastion said as he hung up. He smiled a big, cheesy smile as he thought about her expression upon receiving all those flowers.

*   *   *

"Dr. Scorpeno, you have all the deliveries," an orderly laughed as Autumn approached the desk.

As the nursing staff gathered around the huge collection of flowers, they giggled and smelled the flowers, throwing out comments.

"Ooooo, Doc, you got a serious admirer."

"Doc, you got a man?"

"Doc, somebody is really trying to get and keep your attention." The nursing staff was all over Autumn. She smiled after smelling the many flowers as if each one was new and foreign.

As the nursing staff laughed and said what they'd do to get flowers like this, she politely said to them, "I will be on leave for the next week, so Dr. Picesia will be lead." The nursing staff loved Dr. Scorpeno. They wanted to see her happy, as she put 100 percent of herself to her people and the job.

"Yes, Doc!"

"You go break it all the way down Meg the Stallion/Cardi B style," one of her favorite nurses said as they dispersed back to work.

"Break it down, huh?" Autumn smiled. "I may just do that." She smiled to herself. She had finally found the note in the huge jungle of flowers. "See you soon" it read. A wink emoji seemed to convey what the card's actual words did not. She smelled the card and it didn't smell like him, but she could feel the electricity from the words. A huge smile crept across her face and she imagined what the next week would be like.

"Shit! I have to pack," she said in a hushed voice. She gathered her things, as it was the end of her shift, and headed home. When she finally got in the door, she raced to pack her bags. Over the past week, she and Sasha had built up her Fashion Nova cart with things she thought were sexy and appropriate.

"Girl, you bout to be on this sexy-ass snow trip and you want to buy 'conservative clothes?'" Sasha said making fun of her.

"What do you mean?" Autumn said. "I don't normally wear this stuff. I think it's sexy and you know less thotty than what you put in the cart." Autumn laughed.

"You're right," Sasha said as she made sure to pack all of the kinky underwear and outfits before Autumn could object.

Autumn was getting excited and nervous. " Girl, I'm legitimately going on a trip with this man and I'm not sure how to be or act."

Sasha turned to her friend after holding up some outfits to herself in the mirror. "Look, you deserve some happiness and a little mouth action." Autumn looked playfully shocked as Sasha was talking. "You work too hard and don't take any time for yourself, so hell yeah. Let this man treat you to all the pleasures of Switzerland." They had both laughed and continued to pick through Autumn's closet.

As Sasha was leaving the house for the night she gave her a big huge. "Girl, you go have all the fun. Do all the sightseeing and take all the pictures. But most of all, do all the things you know I'd do."

Autumn laughed and pushed her out the door. "Love you, girl," Autumn said.

"Love you too. Call me when you get there and send me random texts about how things are going. I can live vicariously through you." They laughed again as they parted ways.

Autumn closed the door and headed to bed. *Just the beginning*, she thought as she climbed into bed and got comfortable. She took a deep breath before closing her eyes. "I'm ready," she whispered to the universe as she fell asleep.

Autumn was awake three hours before she needed to be up and felt like she hadn't slept at all. She was too nervous. *Flying on this plane, in these expensive seats is going to be weird*, she thought. She headed out the door, comfortable in her favorite FeedmeFightme leggings, Nikes Free's, her favorite yellow hoodie, and headscarf of tropical colors. Bags in hand and playlist set for the flight, she was ready.

As she arrived at the airport, she was greeted by special employees. "Ms. Scorpeno?"

"Yes?" she said getting out of the car. Suddenly her bags were next to her.

"Hello and welcome. Please follow us this way as we get you to your gate." She was escorted on a special cart that moved her and her luggage swiftly through the airport to her boarding gate.

"Don't I have to check in and check my bags or go through security?" Autumn was worried.

"No, ma'am, your clearances have already been processed and pushed all the way through to your destination. Your bag will be loaded and you will have your carry on brought to you as soon as you are on board," one of the escorts said.

As she scanned her ticket, she looked out the window for a last glance at the city. *Well, Saint Louis, I'll see you in a week.* She boarded the plane and was seated in 3A. It was beautiful. Sitting first class wasn't new, because she treated herself to it on the rare occasions when she took time off, but flying first class on Emirates Airlines was just different. Needless to say, she was pampered on her twelve-hour flight. She had never slept so well and peacefully in her life. The food and drinks were absolutely amazing, and the bathrooms on board were immaculate. It was possibly the best flight she'd ever taken.

As the plane landed, her mind began to wander. *Shit, I didn't call of let him know I had boarded or left or anything.* As she walked toward the baggage claim area, she saw a man dressed in a suit and holding a huge bouquet of flowers. As she got closer to the carousel, she admired the man and the lucky woman he was waiting for. *Damn, that's too cute*, Autumn smiled as she thought of the lucky lady whose man was waiting for her at baggage claim. As she waited for her bags, she listened to her playlist, not paying attention to the man with the huge bouquet of flowers.

"Excuse me, miss?"

Autumn jumped in surprise. "Yes?" she answered.

"I believe these are for you," the man with the flowers brought them down to chest level and there stood Bastion with a huge smile.

Autumn was in shook. "Bastion! OMG! These are beautiful!" she squealed, then threw her arms around his neck as if they were long-distance lovers reuniting.

"Oh! This is nice," Bastion said as he caught her and held her close. He absolutely loved how she smelled. She smelled like honeysuckle flower in the middle of a spring day.

"Oh! Umm, sorry," she blushed, remembering where she was.

Bastion laughed gently and put her down.

"It's so good to see you," she added.

Bastion quickly contained a huge smile. He wanted to be cool around her more stable and secure in himself. When he was around her, he felt all his worries and stressors fade into nothing-ness. Her presence drowned out the life noise because she brought peace to his life.

"Sir, the car awaits," a short, stocky gentleman said, grabbing her bags. As they broke their embrace, he kept hold of her hand felt like a missing piece to the puzzle was finally connected.

As they walked to the car, she noticed it was a Bentley truck. *Oh, my,* she thought. "This is so dope, Bastion," Autumn said quietly.

Bastion smiled at her as he thought about her love for the little things in life.

As they got comfortable in the car, the driver asked, "To the chalet, Mr. Robertson?"

"Yes, Quinton, to the chalet. Thank you so much."

Quinton started the car and they were on the road. "Right away, Mr. Robertson."

As they rode through the mountains, Autumn was fascinated with how beautiful the snow was as it blanketed everything. It was a breathtaking.

"Autumn, I'm so glad you decided to join me," Bastion murmured.

Autumn began to blush as she turned toward him, her cheeks turning a rosy copper color from being cold and then a quick, hot flash coming over her. "Thank you for the beautiful gifts and the, umm, adventure." *Autumn! Adventure, really? Ugh … get it together,* she scolded herself. She was having a mental battle with herself.

Bastion could see she was nervous and even though it was very cute, he wanted her to relax. "Autumn, love, you deserve to see the stars in their most perfect form. I want to have this experience with you. You just have to do a few things for me."

Autumn looked at him, and her eyes widened, then narrowed in suspicion. "Okay, if you getting me to come out here was some kind of game …" she started.

"Autumn!" Bastion interrupted. "I'd never try to trick you or play you in any sort of way. I'm not that kind of guy." He repressed his annoyance and continued to explain. "

Autumn, I want you to relax. I want you to truly feel welcomed and I want you to really enjoy yourself."

She saw his sincerity and realized she was overreacting. "I'm sorry, Bastion. I didn't mean to freak out. This is all really foreign to me and I'm not used to being pampered like this." Autumn grabbed his hand and held it. His grip was gentle yet firm. It felt secure. Autumn's mind immediately went from *Oooo, this is nice* to *I wonder what it feels like when one of his fingers is inside me.* His eyes started to change color as did hers. They had ignited a fire that could burn forever.

"We've arrived, sir," Quinton said as he glided the truck into its parking place.

"Woooow!" Autumn said as she exited the vehicle. "Bastion, this is absolutely beautiful." The chalet was old English-Scot architecture, with the appearance of a castle. As she stared, the high walls and towers covered in snow hypnotized her. Its location on top of a mountain was just the icing on the cake.

Bastion couldn't help but be proud that she seemed to love his style in keeping the chalet's vintage appearance. "Shall we go in? You look cold, love." Bastion ushered her in.

"You're right," Autumn replied, walking into the castle and being greeted by the housekeeper and the butler.

"We'll take your bags, ma'am, and show you to your rooms."

Autumn was overwhelmed with the amount of attention on her. She was also jet lagged, and Bastion could tell. "Stephanie, please run Ms. Autumn a eucalyptus and rose bath in the grand room."

"Right away, sir." Stephanie disappeared immediately and Bastion seemed to be satisfied that he finally had his beautiful phoenix goddess to himself. "How are you feeling, love?"

Not quite hearing him, Autumn turned to find him right behind her, close enough to feel his body heat. "I'm feeling a little sleepy, but I'm okay," she replied, blushing and trying not to stare into his icy blue eyes. Bastion put his hands on her waist and pulled her close.

He smiled down at her smaller but mighty frame and kissed her forehead. "I want you to relax and enjoy yourself." He gently tilted her chin up so he could look into these golden eyes. "Can you promise me that you will relax and do your best not to be stressed?" As he held her gaze, he kissed her slightly open mouth. The heat from her went from simmer to medium-high upon contact with his lips and tongue.

His mouth tastes so good. Autumn could feel the sweat beads forming as they embraced. "Yes," she said as if hypnotized by him.

Unbeknownst to her, he also felt hypnotized. She had a kind of magic he craved … needed.

"Excuse me, sir. The bath has been drawn. Shall I start the playlist you sent over?"

Autumn looked intrigued. "Playlist? Oooh, what playlist?"

Bastion winked at her and said " Go, love. Enjoy your bath and relax for me. You promised." He kissed her on her lips quickly.

Autumn, looking more intrigued, smiled quietly and left with Stephanie.

"Thomas?" He spoke to a young footman who had just turned 100. Sebastion's staff was made up of vampires from the old country who had all been with the family for ages. They had seen Bastion grow from a fledgling to a young, seasoned vampire.

"Yes, sir," Thomas responded.

"Can you call my brother and sister into the parlor for me? I want them to come out and get away for a while."

"Right away, sir."

"Thank you so much."

"What's up, bro?" Royce answered the phone.

"I want to spend some real family time together with you and Mira," Bastion replied. Royce was half asleep and blinded by the phone light. "Tell Mira that you and are coming to see the new observatory with me. You can bring a guest if you want."

"Word" said Royce. "I'm hanging up now."

When Bastion called Mira, she was more than happy to drink and be merry around her brothers. "Shit, little bro, say less," she said.

"We'll see you tomorrow morning," Bastion said, excited to share his love for the stars with not only his brother and sister but possibly the woman of his eternal dreams. As Bastion ended the call with Mira, he headed back to his room. He could hear the smooth sounds of Sade and Maxwell playing in the background over Autumn's voice singing along. *She has such a beautiful voice. She's full of beautiful surprises.* He smiled at the thought of her singing to him while he was inside her. It aroused and pleased him.

"Bastion?" He heard her voice from the bathroom.

"Yes, love?"

"Are you coming in?"

Bastion looked a little surprised as Autumn was normally shy. "Do you want me to bathe with you?"

Autumn was totally relaxed and in her zone. She was completely chilled from the eucalyptus- and rose-infused water and was feeling herself. Autumn thought about him as he asked the question. *I want to know him in so many ways, but I'm nervous.*

"Autumn?"

"Yes…"

Bastion laughed a little. " Is that 'yes' to you want me to come bathe with you?"

Autumn blushed in the already hot water and smiled at the question. "Yes, yes I would," she answered boldly, blushing. Bastion smiled, feeling the energy in the room heat up and relax as she answered the question. "Okay, love. Give me a moment."

Autumn smiled and slid into the tub and under the water. *.I'm being bold!* she squealed internally. She had always wanted to be more like Sasha and confident about who and what she wanted. She wasn't raised like that, though, taught instead to be seen and not heard. Asking Bastion to bathe with her was definitely outside of her comfort zone.

She lifted her head out of the water and wiped the water from her eyes, watching Bastion enter the bathroom. *Good Lord, he looks amazing.* Autumn held her hands over her mouth as she watched him step into the enormous tub.

Bastion smiled as she watched him. "Are you okay?"

Autumn bit her lips under her hands and squealed a little internally. "Yes," she said.

Bastion giggled as he settled into the hot water, getting comfortable. "You seem to be relaxed." He smiled. "I'm glad."

"I am," she said.

He picked her foot up and started to massage it. "Bastion," Autumn said. "Can I ask you something?"

"Anything, love."

She took a deep breath and asked, "What made you want to invite me here? Don't get me wrong, I love all this, but I'm kind of apprehensive.

Bastion looked down at the beautiful foot he held in his hand and smiled as the steam rose around them. "Autumn, I told you I wanted to prove to you that I can and will give you everything you deserve if you took a chance on me. This is just a token of my thanks because you decided to take that chance and I'm very grateful." Bastion looked up with those icy blue eyes from the tiny foot he was massaging.

Autumn blushed and smiled. She enjoyed her feet being touched and rubbed, but also because he was damn near perfect. As the bath continued, they talked about everything from traveling to their favorite music. Surprisingly they had a lot in common and they seemed open to trying the interests they didn't already share.

"Well, I guess we should get out of here and, ummm, get ready for bed," Autumn finally said.

Bastion flashed a devilish smile as he kissed her foot gently. He looked like the most beautiful sin. "Yes, we should."

Autumn had turned the hue of a ripe peach as she sat in the tub with Bastion and despite how long they had sat in the tub, the water never cooled. In fact, it seemed to get warmer as they talked.

"I'll get out first and be off to my room for the night," Autumn said as she rose from the tub. The maid had left a beautiful black-and-gold floral patterned robe near the tub. The towels were the thickest but lightest things she'd ever felt. *Wow, these feel amazing*, she thought as she faced away from Bastion. She dried herself off slowly, as she felt she was being watched but didn't want to turn around for fear of falling that much more in love with this man.

Bastion was indeed watching her dry her silky, golden skin and it turned him on. His eyes seem to glow an icy blue as his eyelids slid slightly closed. He could watch his beautiful golden-brown angel forever. "Umm, this robe is gorgeous," she said, distracting herself.

"I'm pleased you like it. I wanted you to feel free and comfortable for the entire time you were here." Bastion leaned over the tub of the tube with his arms folded, watching her drop her towel and put the robe on. *Oh my,* he thought as he breathed very slowly and deeply. He could see every flex of her muscles. *Her skin and tattoos ... She's a walking masterpiece I must keep pristine.* She slid the robe on and tied the belt around her waist. It was long enough to cover her peach bottom and fell to her knees. It felt perfect. Bastion's fangs began to ache as she modeled and admired the robe in the floor-to-ceiling mirror as he thought of her naked under the robe.

As she turned in the mirror, she looked over her shoulder to find Bastion's gaze and fangs zeroed in on her. She smiled a naughty smile over her shoulder and let the robe drop a little off her naked shoulder. Bastion saw this and let out a low, primal growl. Autumn blushed, feeling her temperature rise and her juices start to gather. "Bastion," she murmured, gathering her foggy thoughts.

"Yes, love," he said, rising out of the tub. He looked like a long-lost god of the sea with his long hair slicked back, and his fangs and eyes seemed to glow as he got closer to her.

"Bastion," she whispered. He was right on top of her. She had backed against the marble sink counter.

"Yes, my love," he whispered. "Talk to me, Autumn." He could see the beads of sweat begin to accumulate on her exposed chest tattoo. It was beautiful.

"I ... um ... You ...," Autumn stuttered.

Bastion was staring into her golden eyes and began to touch her waist. His fingers danced around her hip tattoos as the made their way to the small of her back. "Yes, Autumn?" Bastion kept his eyes focused on hers. His fangs were fully extended now.

She began to arch her back, feeling her pussy juices dripping from her arousal. "Kiss me," she whispered breathlessly as he gently pulled her closer to his naked body. Bastion lifted her on to the counter and kissed her waiting mouth gently and deeply. She opened her mouth and slid her tongue against his.

"Uggghh," Bastion moaned. He held the small of her back as he pulled her closer to him. She opened her legs to feel his dick at the entrance to her ocean. As they enjoyed each other's taste, Bastion gently tugged her robe and let it fall around her voluptuous hips.

Her naked, tattooed body was flawless. She was everything he ever wanted, but most important she was what he absolutely needed. She ignited a fire in him he'd never felt before with anyone. His member grew at these thoughts.

She could feel him at her opening as she spread her legs further. His kiss felt like the sweetest part of heaven and she was hypnotized. They were both feverish from the energy they created together. The steam in the bathroom seemed to thicken as they continued to touch and kiss each other. Bastion pulled her closer to him and felt himself at the cusp of ecstasy. Autumn took a breath as she felt his length begin to push into her sheath.

Bastion kissed down her beautifully tempting neck. Autumn was moving on auto pilot, her body's cry for release overshadowing her mind whisper to waiting or any hint of apprehension. Her body was in control and she was along for the anticipated, glorious ride. Bastion readied himself to enter her ocean.

"Uggghh Bastion," Autumn moaned as he began to drive deeper into her.

"Autumn, my love. You're so tight," he whispered as he kissed and drove deeply into her. She wrapped her arms and legs around him, as he thrust deeply into her.

"Bastion … oooohhh…," she moaned again.

"Hold on to me," he instructed. He had was so entranced by the way she felt and tasted that he had to get into a better position to fully enjoy their first time together. He carried her with ease to his bed. It was covered with the finest of Egyptian-cotton sheets and blankets. The enormous canopy bed looked like something from medieval times. She was too entranced to take account of the beauty of it as she was wanting more of him. Still rock hard inside her, he laid her down on the bed and looked down at her gorgeous body. She was perfect in every way.

He loved every inch of her, from her intellect to her naivete. He loved both her boldness and her shyness, and her conservative wildness. *I love … her. Oh my god … I love her.* The revelation was like a light switch turning on in Bastion's mind. He'd been in the dark for so long that the fire she emits lights up his world.

"Bastion? Is something wrong?" Autumn looked a little worried by his expression.

Bastion, realizing he was balls deep inside, her snapped back into this beautiful fantasy come to life. "No, my love." He kissed her deeply. "Everything is perfect." He smiled into her mouth and began to rock back and forth as they kissed. Soon they were oblivious to this world and faded into each other's universe.

*　　*　　*

"Royce! If death had a timetable for you, I swear you'd be late for it," Mira snarled. "Let's go! Jones already said he plane was ready!"

"Damn, Mira, I swear you're worse than a mom. You're like a wife named Karen!" Royce and Mira argued all the way to the car. They loved each other, but without Bastion there to act as their referee they were at each other the whole time.

"We've arrived at the plane, Ms. Mira."

"Thank you, Jones. Please make sure the house is taken care of while we are gone and, as always, give me a call if you need anything."

"Yes, ma'am," Jones said as he and his helper removed the luggage from the trunk. Royce was at the plane already and was FacetTming Bastion to inform him they were about to be on their way. "What up, bro? What'cha doing?" Royce said in his usual over-exaggeratedly loud voice.

Bastion replied with a whispered, "What's up yourself?"

Royce's eyes widened, then he squinted and smirked. "Oh … I know what you're doing." He laughed out loud.Bastion was creeping out of his room, leaving his beautiful curly haired golden angel. She was peacefully sleeping and he wanted to just watch her sleep, but had to answer his phone.

"Shut up, bitch," Bastion replied, blushing. "Soooo, is the good doctor there and you just got a dose of … shall we say … some good medicine?" Royce replied.

"First of all, bitch…," Bastion finally spoke louder as he had reached the living room and was wearing basketball shorts. "Yes, she is here and mind your own fucking business."

Royce burst out laughing as Mira walked up.

"Hey, little bro," Mira said , seeing his face. "You look relaxed," she noted.

Royce laughed again and said, "Yeah, he does," then winked at his brother.

Bastion ignored Royce's antics and gave his sister a warm smile.

"Bastion, we aren't bringing anybody with us, but I want to warn you," Mira looked serious. "Cat called me as I was packing and asked what I was up to. I told her we were on our way to see you as the new observatory in Switzerland."

" Ugh! Come on, Mira!"

Mira looked stressed. "I'm sorry Bastion. I wasn't lying and I didn't know I wasn't supposed to say anything."

Bastion looked at his sister's angelic face, distorted from his disappointment. "It's all good, Mira. It's not like she's going to show up or anything. At least I hope not."

Royce, too, looked disappointedly at Mira. "What, Royce?" Mira looked annoyed by her brother.

"Girl, you know Bastion hates that girl."

Mira pushed him hard and said, "Shut up and get on the plane, stupid."

Royce, still looking disappointed and unfazed by his sister's push, turned back to Bastion. "Aight bro, we'll see you in a few hours."

"Word. Y'all be safe."

They hung up and Bastion pinched the bridge of his nose and closed his eyes in frustration. *Ugh. That bitch would show up too just be to annoying and ruin what I have planned*, he thought. *Nope, I'm going to enjoy my family time and spend this week enjoy my beautiful treasure. She deserves this as much as I do*, he resolved. Bastion had made the decision to not be upset. He had the most beautiful creature in the universe in his bed and his family was on their way. The more he thought about the positives, the faster he returned to his happy place. As he sat on the over-sized plush couch, he watched the snow falling against the night sky. It was mesmerizing. Then he heard his bedroom door open and the gentle footsteps of an angel get closer to him. *Gods, she is beautiful.* Her hair was down and fell over her shoulders in golden curls. She walked quietly up to him and wrapped her arms around his neck as she curled up on his lap. She had put her robe on, covering her curves since they weren't entirely alone in the house, but wore nothing else.

He kissed her head as she settled into him like she was made for his lap. She was warm, like softened caramel dripping over golden-brown skin. She was so beautiful. It was unreal.

"What are you up to, handsome?" she said as she smiled and kissed his chest.

He took a deep breath and closed his eyes, as her kisses were all the fuel he needed to get going again. "I was watching the snow fall and talking to my brother and sister."

She continued to kiss him as she talked "How are they?"

Bastion, now semi hard, struggled reply. "Umm, they are fine. They are on their way here to join us for the observatory opening."

Autumn, sat up looking kind of nervous. Bastion opened his eyes and searched her face. She looked worried.

"Oh, okay. Will I be intruding on family time?" she asked nervously, feeling slightly disappointed. Somewhere deep inside she had expected this to happen. *Some things just weren't meant to be. Why did I even come?*

Bastion could see the wheels turning in her head. "No, Not at all. You are my priority, Autumn. Listen. Hear me when I say this," Bastion sweetly lifted her face to his. "I promised you the stars and I will give them to you. I told you I wanted to show you I am worthy of your love and I will do absolutely anything to never let you forget that." Autumn, carefully listening to him, began to relax again.

He held her tense body close to him as he kissed her forehead and cradled her in his lap. She wanted to fall head over heels for him, but she was scared. She had never experienced these kinds of emotions all at once before. She was beginning to become emotionally invested in him. *Deep breath, Autumn. Relax and enjoy this galactic ride.* She took another deep breath against his chest and felt safe, safe enough to fall asleep on him. The surrounding space was silent and only their energy was present. Beautifully electric and calming energy flowed around them. Bastion felt the heat from her body temperature increase dramatically, and soon a warm yellow and orange glow began to appear.

Bastion looked around them and what he saw amazed him. The room glowed with a soft golden light and kind of sparkled against the night sky. He looked down at Autumn, who was fast asleep. She was glowing. Her skin lit up slowly and her tattoos looked like she was covered in lines of gold, red, and orange. Her hair had started to twinkle, as if tiny white Christmas lights were interlaced from the roots to the ends. He smiled brightly now. He held her a little tighter and she snuggled into his chest. *She's a real phoenix. My dream was right.* All of his memories of what the lore said about them appeared to be absolutely true.

She was at peace in his arms and she was solidified in his heart. *She's the one. She's my very own mythical goddess. She's mine,* Bastion thought as he held his queen and watched the snow fall.

*   *   *

"Bastion! What up, little bro! Good to see you!" Royce greeted him. Bastion was in the foyer waiting for his brother and sister to arrive. He gave his sister a hug and dapped up his brother.

"Bastion, you really look relaxed and happy. What's going on?" Mira demanded.

Royce laughed as he was helping Thomas bring their bags in.

"I am, Mira. For the first time in a very long time I am," Bastion replied.

Mira smiled and hugged her brother as they finally made their way to the living room. As Mira and Royce got comfortable, Autumn appeared.

"Oh! Hello Dr. Scorpeno. What are you doing up here?" Mira asked, looking confused.

Royce's eyes were wide and a huge Cheshire-cat smile crept across his face.

As Autumn was about to reply, Bastion walked in. "Mira, Royce, you remember Autumn."

"Yes, it's very nice to see you again," Mira responded politely, still looking confused.

Royce, still smiling like a goofy kid, shook her hand. "Yes, very nice to see you again, Autumn."

Bastion saw Royce's expression and panicked. Mira, too, was looking at Bastion, waiting for an explanation. "Autumn, will you excuse us, love?"

"Sure," Autumn said awkwardly.

As she left the room, Bastion turned toward his sister, who had her arms folded, and his brother with his hands in his pockets. "So, explain Bastion," Mira looked intensely at her brother.

"Yeah Bastion, explain," Royce mocked his sister's stance with a smile on his face.

"I invited Autumn here because I really like her and I want to show her I'm the man for her."

"Really, Bastion? Honey, you don't know her?" Mira said in her mom voice. Royce stood behind his sister's back, mocking her.

"Listen, Mira. I really like Autumn and I want to be with her. She's different from any other woman I've ever been with and she means everything to me. I believe I love her and that she's of the lore."

"How do you know?" Mira was still not convinced, and Royce was absolutely giddy with laugher.

"Yeah, Bastion! How do you know?" Royce echoed Mira.

"Mira, just trust me and let me live."

"Fine," Mira said, clearly not happy about this unexpected revelation. "I just want you to be happy, Bastion. But I know you'll make good decisions, unlike someone else." She looked pointedly at Royce.

"Wow, Mira. Really? That's all Bastion gets?"

"Yes!" Mira turned toward Royce.

Royce rolled his eyes and walked past her to give his brother a hug. "As long as you're happy, bro. For real. Tell me though, was the dosage just the right amount?"

Bastion burst out laughing and punched his brother. As they talked about family business and laughed at each other, Autumn was FaceTiming Sasha.

"Hey girl. What's up? How's the geeky/kinky week going?" Sasha giggled and winked.

Autumn laughed at her friend and smiled. " It was going great until his family showed up."

"Bitch, what? They showed up unexpectedly? That's not good," Sasha said, looking concerned.

"Well, he invited them so he could spend time with them and they could get to know me, I guess."

Sasha pouted. "Really? Still sounds weird to me."

"It was and is," Autumn said sadly.

"Well, babe, you'll be okay. Bastion still wants to be all up in your cookies, right?"

"Bitch, shut up!" Autumn laughed.

Sasha laughed too. "I'm just saying, hun, enjoy this time with him and get to know his family. Shit, if I could I'd come out and distract Royce for you. Yass, hunty," Sasha said.

"Well, would you be opposed to coming out for real?" Autumn wasn't joking. "Girl, you serious?"

"Yeah?" Autumn was almost pleading.

"Shit yeah, bitch! I'm on the way!"

Autumn was overjoyed and kind of relieved her friend was flying to Europe to keep her from struggling with being alone.

"Let's go out and see the sights, love!" Bastion said, seeing Autumn sitting cross-legged on his bed.

"I just FaceTimed with Sasha and I invited her to join us," Autumn announced.

Bastion looked confused. "Okay. Are you alright? Did I make you feel uncomfortable with my family coming here?" Autumn grabbed his hand and lifted it to her face. He felt that warm caramel feeling, which he loved.

"I asked her to come because that way I won't feel alone, and if you guys are conducting family business then I won't be alone in a strange country with strange people around me."

Bastion thought about it for a minute and understood her concerns. "You're right, my love. I shall arrange for her to get here as soon and safely as possible. Your happiness is everything to me, and I don't want you to ever question it."

"Thank you, Bastion! I lo— thank you, love." Autumn caught herself almost saying she loved him.

Whew, that was super close, she thought, looking shocked and blushing slightly. Bastion winked and smiled , then kissed her shy smile in understanding. "You're always welcome, my beautiful Nubian goddess."

Sasha walked toward the baggage claim and saw a dapper older man accompanied by a younger gentleman. The younger one held a sign with her name on it. "Hello, I'm Sasha."

Quinton matched her face to the picture Bastion had given him. "Hello, Ms. Sasha. Please step this way." As Quinton walked her toward the exit, Thomas ran back to get her bag.

"Mr. Quinton!" The older gentleman stopped in his tracks. That voice was one he recognized and hated. Quinton motioned to Thomas to take Ms. Sasha to the car and start it..

"Hello, Ms. Ortega. How may I help you?" Quinton didn't care for the Ortega family, but most of all hated Catherine and her Brother Zepher. They were the worst kind of vampire royalty. They felt entitled to rule over all creatures of the lore. True, their family was one of the first vampire families, but that didn't give them the right to be nasty to everyone they encountered. She strolled up to him, her entourage in tow.

"You can help me by telling me who that was and why you are escorting her around."

Quinton was perturbed by her tone and question. "Respectfully, Ms. Ortega, that's not my business nor is it yours. Good-bye." Quinton dismissed himself.

Catherine was not pleased with that answer and growled at him. Her eyes become black as night and her claws extended. "Are you lying to me, Mr. Quinton?"

Quinton looking unfazed and confidently said, "No, ma'am. I am not. If you'll excuse me, I bid you farewell."

As Quinton turned toward the door and began to walk away, Catherine scratched his back. He dropped to the ground, but held his tongue. "Don't ever turn your back on me. You'll get killed doing that," she said with a crazed, fanged smile before she turned to walk away. "Good evening, Mr. Quinton," she said over her shoulder. Her assistant looked back at him then gave her a handkerchief to wipe her hands. She threw it on the ground and kept walking toward her own transportation.

"What a bitch," Quinton said, getting up and going out to the truck.

"Mr. Quinton! What happened?" Thomas asked, looking nervous. Sasha looked apprehensive as well. "Nothing this old man can't use some brandy and some cotton swabs to fix," Quinton replied. "Let's get you out of this cold and to your friend."

Thomas and Sasha still looked nervous, but less now that they were driving toward the destination.

Gotta warn the family about the psychopath being here, Quinton thought as he drove up to the chalet.

"Biiihhhh! Hey boooo!" Sasha yelled as she hopped out the truck and hugged her friend.

"Hey boo!" Autumn smiled widely as she hugged her friend.

"Oooo girl! This castle is mad dope!" Sasha was amazed at the site of the chalet.

"I know, right. Come on in!" Autumn said.

"Welcome to Switzerland, Sasha," Bastion said, smiling as he appeared behind Autumn.

"Well, hello Bastion. How are you?" Sasha smiled as she looked back and forth between the two.

Autumn blushed and whispered, "Shut up!" Sasha laughed at her as she walked past.

"Well, well, well. I knew Switzerland had some of the world's best desserts, but it looks like someone imported some spicy caramel just for me," Royce said as he caught sight of Sasha's caramel curves. "Why hello Sasha. Welcome to Switzerland."

"Hey Royce, don't you look just as gorgeous as when I saw you last," she replied.

Autumn looked at her friend as she was distracted by Royce and laughed a little. She felt more at home as her best friend and sister had come halfway around the world to be with her.

Bastion felt her body temperature increase as he hugged her from behind. "Are you happy, my love?" he whispered into she neck. He loved the smell of her. She smelled like jasmine and honeysuckle and he just wanted to drink of her forever.

Her body contoured to his as she melted into him. "I am love. I am." She turned around and wrapped her arms around his back, rose up on her toes, and kissed him deeply. He held her close, picked her up, and soaked up her essence.

* * *

Catherine was deep in thought as she was being driven to her own mansion. *What does a girl have to get everything? I deserve everything, damn it.*" Her mind was going a mile a minute.

"Ms. Catherine," a voice broke into her thoughts. "We've arrived." Catherine sighed, then opened the door and took an arm to escort her to the door.

"Hello, Ms. Catherine, welcome. Shall we start your bath?"

"Absolutely," Catherine said as walked into the dimly lit house. It was fitted with the most modern fixtures and furniture and was extremely rigid and cold. She loved it. She loved how straightforward and bold it was.

Catherine had everything, yet she couldn't have the man she desired most. She was getting upset. As she walked into her glamorous bedroom, she looked at herself. She stood just under six feet tall and was pale and blond. She was, literally, drop-dead gorgeous. She was 1000 years old and didn't look a day over twenty-five. She was made an immortal at that age and looked that age ever since.

Sebastion doesn't know what he is missing in me. I may have tormented him a time or two, but who doesn't do that to a new fledgling? She laughed at all of the horrible things she had done to him. She remembered a particularly amusing time when she had forced Sebastion to kill someone he loved.

"You need to eat, Sebastion," Catherine laughed.

"Why would you do this to me?" Sabastion pleaded.

"Come now, Bastion, my love. You are a new vampire on the brink of starvation. She was just a meal. You no longer get to choose what you eat and, unfortunately for her, she caught you at the wrong time." Catherine found his suffering brought her pleasure and become quite addicted to it. She found that she got the best pleasure out of it because he destroyed his meals and was still crazed. She then went full vampire and they fucked uncontrollably, covered in the victim's blood. It was still her ultimate fantasy.

It was perfect until he found an alternative to taking only human blood. He had become strong in his resolutions for cleaner living and now only occasionally drank from a human. Never enough to kill them, but they'd be in a deep, coma-like sleep until the next morning. They wouldn't remember anything, and their puncture marks would be gone with the morning sun. Once she realized she could no longer control Sebastion, she lost it. She went into full rage mode and tried to provoke him. But by then Sebastion had had enough of her shit. Remembering all of the abuse she had inflicted upon him, he finally reached his breaking point and raged out on her.

His fangs had grown abnormally long and razor sharp as his body grew instantly. His eyes were as black as obsidian and his claws extended, ready to maul her to death. Never one to prefer the defensive, she lunged toward him and he dodged her attack. He was extremely fast. She was surprised and, oddly, enjoying this. "So, you've grown into yourself now!" she hissed.

Sebastion snarled and growled, "Come find out, bitch!" He wasn't scared of what she'd do to him, but what he might do to her.

She lunged at him again. This time she made contact and sliced through his shirt across his chest. "Not fast enough," Catherine taunted.

Bastion looked down at his chest, saw his own blood, and became even more enraged. Catherine took another run at him, looking to slit his throat, but Bastion grabbed her instead mid leap. With his bone-crushing grip on her throat, he slammed her into the floor. Catherine was still kicking and snapping at him, but he squeezed his hand around her throat even more tightly.

"Stop it you stupid bitch!" Catherine, slowly losing consciousness, hissed, "Never, you fucking bitch!"

He grip tightened, and her kicks slowed, then stopped as her hands dropped.

Sebastion saw she was losing consciouness and released his grip. She coughed and sucked in air. Vampires don't need to breathe, but the body continues to do it as a reflex. Sebastion was breathing heavily as Catherine rose, trying to confront him again. She couldn't keep her balance, and fell again to the floor.

"We're fucking done Catherine. You're a crazy-ass bitch and I don't ever want to have anything to do with yo ass again. Period."

Catherine cackled, still recovering from almost getting her neck broken. "You can't quit me, you pussy-ass bitch! Nobody quits me. I'll let you go when I'm good and fucking ready!"

Bastion walked toward the door of her house, her screamed obscenities still ringing in his ears. "Sebastion! Bring your stupid ass back here! Do you hear me? Don't walk away from me, Bitch!"

Bastion walked out of the house and never looked back.

"Aw Sebastion, we had such good times, love," Catherine said to herself as she sat in her bath. Then she thought about the most recent time she'd seen him, in New Orleans when she watched him laugh with that mortal black bitch. Catherine snarled, her lips over her fangs, as she thought about how that bitch made him smile and laugh.

"How can you love a fucking mortal, Sebastion? Disgusting. What can she do for you that I couldn't? No matter. Soon, Sebastion, you won't have her to make you smile. When it's time, you'll know who really loves you and will come back to me." Catherine smiled a truly sinister smile. She was as savage as she was beautiful. She was truly deadly, and wasn't afraid to let those she felt were beneath her know.

"Ms. Catherine, would you like us to inform Ms. Mira of your arrival?"

Catherine thought about it and that horribly sinister smile appeared again. "No." She smiled, her fangs extended. "No, thank you. It's a surprise." Catherine laughed out loud to herself as she continued to bathe. " Yesss, that's it. A surprise indeed."

"B! Let's take the ladies out for some drinks and dinner. They've never been here and I'm trying to flaunt my spicy caramel treat around the town, you know what I'm saying?" Royce said, waggling his eyebrows as he bursting into Bastion's room. Autumn, dressing, shrieked with surprise.

"Damn it, Royce!" Bastion ran out of his closet in just his drawers. "How about you fucking knock first, dickhead!"

Royce stood there with his hands over his eyes and laughed. "Damn, bro! My bad! I apologize, Autumn." Royce was truly an idiot, but he had a great heart.

"Okay Royce, get your ass out of here. Fuck!" Bastion was blocking Royce from seeing any more of Autumn as he pushed him out the door..

"I'll get Sasha all hot and bothered and then we'll be ready."

"Okay, Bitch, go!"

Royce laughed as he was shoved out the door. "Sorry again, Autumn!" he yelled over his shoulder.

Autumn laughed as she began to relax. "Your brother is something else."

Bastion standing by the door, locking it this time, turned and moved to help her zip up her dress. "Yes, indeed, he is." Bastion smiled and admired the way the zipper inched up her back.

Autumn was wearing a yellow bandage dress, one of the outfits she brought thanks to Sasha.

"Goddamn, love. You look absolutely delicious," Bastion said. His fangs began to extend as he ran his hands around her waist and held her hips. He could smell her arousal as she pushed her peachy booty into his semi-hard dick.

"I'm glad you like it, love." Autumn stared and smiled as she eye fucked him. His eyes were that icy blue and he certainly felt like he was ready.

Bastion growled, picked her up, and carried her to the freshly made bed. Autumn laughed and playfully protested. "Bae, we've going to be late for dinner!"

Bastion looked down as his gorgeous queen. He slid his hand between her wet and sticky thighs and inserted two fingers into her warm pussy. "Oh, Bastion!" she whimpered.

"I'm okay with having being late to dinner when I can have my dessert now."

She looked up at him with glowing gold eyes and he continued to stroke the inside of her pussy. "Bastion, " she said, breathing heavily.

"Yes, my love," he said, stroking her pussy and kissing her body.

"My makeup and hair will be ruined, honey," she said in an attempt to not get too wild. Bastion laughed at his queen's pleas for gentle loving. She was so independent and he loved it. He continued to kiss her and offered her an alternative to being dicked all the way down.

He slid his fingers from her pussy.

"Oh no, what's wrong?" Autumn whispered.

"Nothing, my love." Bastion smiled. He held her hands to his chest and kissed them.

Autumn looked suspicious." Okay?" she said, giving him a curious glance.

Bastion smiled that devilishly handsome smile and gently pushed her arms above her head. "Hold them up there."

Autumn looked more curious, as Bastion kept eye contact the whole time. He kissed down her mid-length dress till he met the top of her thighs. "Bastion," she whined.

"Shhhh, my love. Let me enjoy my dessert and I promise you will, too." Bastion kissed her thighs as he lifted her dress and spread her juicy thighs apart.

The delicious aroma of honeysuckle and jasmine made his mouth water and his dick rock hard. He could see her clit was dripping and he licked the sides of her thighs where her juices dripped. "Mmmm, yes, my sweet angel. You taste so fucking good." He slipped a finger back into her and her back arched.

"UGGGGHH, Bastion!" He laughed a little. Bastion was enjoying his queen in the most intimate way and he loved it. To hear his name out of her mouth was like the most beautiful hymn he'd ever heard. She was so entranced that she was starting to close her legs. "No, no, my naughty siren. You'll give me what I came for, my love." He pushed her legs apart gently and held them apart this time.

"Bastion, I need to take my panties off first, love."

He laughed again as he leaned into her and kissed her pussy with his fangs. Pop! He snapped the tiny piece of lace separating her naked pussy from his entire mouth. He threw the torn pair of Fenty-Savage panties across the room. Bastion looked back at the waiting, open pussy of his

Nubian queen. "I love that brand … I'll buy you more later," he said, in a hurry to get back to his meal.

"Bastion, I need you," Autumn moaned in her sultry voice. She began to touch her pussy, getting hotter by the second.

Bastion leaned into to kiss her hands, then grabbed them and pushed them up to her head. His fangs were fully extended and his ice-blue eye were bent on devouring her pussy. "Don't move them down here again my love," he ordered seductively. When Autumn complied, he continued, "That's my beautiful Nubian queen."

Bastion kissed up her right thigh. Her juices were so thick and sticky, like the sweetest honey from the garden of Eden. He let his tongue trace his name all the way up to her pussy lips. Right before he dove in, he stopped and kissed the left thigh the same way.

This was driving Autumn crazy. She felt like time had stopped as he played with her mind and body. "Bastion, please," she cried.

Bastion smiled into her pussy lips as he gently kissed them and finger fucked her. "Tell me what you want my love. Talk to me, my queen." Bastion spoke to her pussy lips and was making them talk back.

"Please, Bastion, let me cum."

"As you wish, my gorgeous creature." As he breathed those words into her, he gripped her hips and brought her pussy to his mouth.

The way he dove, tongue deep, into her she almost creamed all over his face. "Bastion!" she screamed through her hands, covering her mouth for fear the whole house would hear her being devoured. Bastion was intoxicated by the taste of her juices. He scratched her clit with one of his fangs. "Oh! Oh my god! Bastion! What was that?" she cried. She wanted to say stop, but it felt too good. Bastion locked her thighs down and she couldn't squirm away. The more she moved, the more the scratch bleed. Her blood and pussy juices were the missing links in his DNA. The taste was indescribable. She tasted of heaven and hell, spicy and sweet … fuck! She was everything.

"Bastion! I'm going to cum!" she moaned, exhausted from being sexually paralyzed.

"Cum for me, my love," he instructed, torn between drinking her life essence and beating himself off.

"Ooooo, ooooooo…Oh my god! Ugghhhhh!" Her body convulsed, gave a last burst of energy, and she burst into flames. Bastion loved it! Her energy was intense, so intense she caused the lights in the house to brighten then blow a fuse. Enjoying the light show, Bastion blew his load in his hand, then slowed his pace and took a few deep breaths. Autumn's body was done. She had sweated her hair out and her makeup had run everywhere.

Bastion took a towel from the bathroom and wiped the thighs of his now barefaced beauty. He crawled over her, kissing her deeply as he fell next to her on the bed.

Autumn felt light as a cloud. She felt drained and recharged at the same time. She finally opened her eyes and saw the lights were out. "What happened to the lights?" she murmured.

Bastion looked at her, surprised, and laughed softly. "Bae, you did that."

"What do you mean I did that?"

Bastion was perplexed, but let it go for now. He thought this was interesting, as she really didn't know she was a mythical creature. She took a deep breath and lay there, still in her bliss. "You're amazing, Autumn, I hope you know this, my love."

She yawned and said, "You, too, Bastion." Still in a blissful afterglow, she curled up next to him and mumbled, "I love you."

Bastion's hearing perked up as he rubbed her hair and asked her to repeat what she said. "What was that, love? Autumn?" Bastion looked down, but she was fast asleep.

A knock at the door caused Bastion to groan. "Shit," he murmured before gently moving himself from under Autumn and walking to the door. It was Royce.

"What's up?" Bastion asked.

Royce saw his brother looking disheveled and laughed at him.

Bastion wasn't fooling with him and began to shut the door. " Okay! Damn bro, Chill."

"What do you want?" Bastion asked, annoyed.

"Yo, so we aren't going out since the power went out and they are working to get it back up."

"Okay," Bastion was pushing the door closed.

" Okay! Damn bro, chill." Royce repeated.

Bastion calmed down and laughed at himself, realizing his patience had gotten thin with people trying to keep him from being close to Autumn for any reason.

"Have a great night anyway, bro. Catch y'all in the morning. Maybe." Royce winked at his brother.

"Goodnight bro!" Bastion hugged his brother and pushed him out before

closing and locking the door. "So, the power is out for the night. That means no heat." He looked Autumn's fully clothed, sleeping body and loved everything about it. He kissed her and woke her gently.

"Are we going out?" she yawned.

He smiled at her beautifully sleepy face and said, "No, my love. The power was knocked out across the city, so we are going to chill here and try it again later."

Autumn pulled off her dress and looked for her nightgown. "I think my nightgowns are being washed." She blushed, as she hadn't spent the night with Bastion yet. They had taken a bath together and had the most wonderful sex she had ever had in her life. But lying in his bed and falling asleep next to him was a little scary.

"I have a tee shirt you can wear, if you like," he offered.

She looked shy and turned a peachy color. He now knew this was her happy phase. "Can I, please?" She looked down as her eyes flashed a golden glow and her blush became brighter.

"Absolutely, my love. You never have to ask for anything. Tell me what you need and I will provide it for you." Bastion handed her one of his t-shirts.

"Thank you, love." Autumn put the t-shirt on, and it was crazy long on her. It came down to her knees, but it hugged all of her curves just right. She hugged him tightly and he could feel her body heat rise again.

"Are you ready for bed, darling?" he asked.

She yawned, and her sleepy golden eyes caught his ice-blue ones in a hypnotic trance.

"Yes," she whispered and he swept her up in his arms. He sat her gently on the bed and she shimmied up to the head of the bed and squirmed her way under the heavy winter blankets.

"Your bed is so big and comfortable," she said with a sleepy smile.

He stood by the bed, looking down at her for a minute or two. He watched her get comfortable and, as he did, he felt his heart come alive. He felt it beat for the first time in 600 years. He had found his soul mate. She finally stopped squirming, turned toward him, and patted the bed. "Come lay with me, Bastion. Keep me warm." She smiled with her eyes closed.

"Forever, Autumn." He climbed into bed and she burrowed herself into his body. She was finally comfortable and fell fast asleep. "Forever I will keep you safe and you'll keep us warm. Goodnight, my beautiful phoenix queen."

They slept so peacefully. Together their magic let them drift off into galactic bliss. They sailed the stars and moons of their own slumber land.

*　　*　　*

Time seemed to both stand still and fly by as the week went on. Autumn and Bastion played tourist in Switzerland and saw as much as they possibly could. Bastion was very much familiar with the city, but the energy he received from Autumn as she enjoyed every moment of this adventure hit him differently. He'd never taken a trip for relaxation, let alone with a woman who made him feel more then he ever had in his 600 years of eternal life. He was absolutely in love. Tonight he would tell her under the stars.

"I'm nervous, Bastion," Autumn said, standing in her new Savage X Fenty underwear in the bathroom. She didn't let men buy her things normally, but this past week Bastion hadn't allowed her to purchase or pay for anything. She had tried a few times on the sly when they were out to dinner, but the waitstaff had indicated that the bill was already covered and then some. It was extremely foreign to her. Bastion smiled his beautifully devilish smile to himself in the floor-to-ceiling mirror in his room. He had stepped out of his closet in an all-black custom-made Balenciaga suit designed by Martine Rose.

Bastion was drop-dead gorgeous, Autumn thought. *Like Yung Joc said, "Fresh to death everyday like he jumped up out a casket." Fine.*

"I'm more then positive that you look absolutely stunning, lover," Bastion reassured her. They had spent so much time together, it seemed so natural. *It felt like that was how it should have been all along*, he thought to himself. He had felt it. Everything felt so natural with her. He had to wonder how had he gone half a millennium without this feeling, the feeling of real happiness and joy. The feeling of peace, whole and complete.

"Ugh, that doesn't make me feel any less nervous, Bastion."

He laughed a little, as he found her nervousness and innocence as beautiful as she was. For such a confident woman who didn't let anyone do anything for her, she was nervous over the smallest things. "Autumn, sweetheart, I promise you are and will be the most beautiful woman at the gala, my love."

Autumn finally slipped on the long-awaited sequined Vera Wang gown Bastion had given her for this event. How did you know my size? OMG!" The dress was beautiful and form fitting. It was a stunning, deep yellow color with ombre hues of orange and red, flowing to the floor. A slit that reached halfway up her thigh, and at the back was very low cut.

Autumn looked phenomenal. Bastion had never seen her hair straightened, and it had been a long while since she had done it. She was proud of her crown of curls, but tonight she wanted to really glam up. *He better appreciate this*, she laughed to herself. To prepare for the event, Sasha and Autumn had gone out with Mira for a girl's day. They had a blast, laughing about things from family to school to life in general. Surprisingly, Mira had a lot in common with both girls and that made Autumn feel welcomed, in case things got serious with Bastion.

Bastion and Royce enjoyed brother time as they picked up their suits. Royce told Bastion of all the nasty sex things he and Sasha had and would do. Bastion side eyed his brother, but laughed as he could see that he was really feeling Sasha. Royce was ridiculous, but Bastion loved his brother just the same. When they finally got back to the house, it was time to get dressed. Royce had finally quit sneaking back and forth to Sasha's guest room and they were staying in the same room. It was easier on them and the rest of the house, rather than stumble through the house in the middle of the night for some loving.

"Okay, I think I'm ready," Autumn finally said as she put on the last of her Juvia's Place lipstick. She was damn near perfect. Her make-up slapped so hard and she wore her favorite, special-occasion, had-it-for-five-years, one-spray-every-six-months Dolce and Gabbana *The One* perfume. She loved the way it smelled and how it seemed to make her feel more powerful and sexy.

It heightened her sexual prowess and her confidence to knowing she was that bitch. She smiled and blew a kiss to herself, then walked out, popping her red bottoms. Bastion was finishing a quick bow on a thin box when he looked up and saw his personal heaven. He completely froze.

"Well, what do you think?" Autumn flashed a devastating smile at him as she did a sassy twirl to show off everything from her super-long, natural high ponytail to her gift-wrapped, incredibly beautiful curves, to her perfectly fit black-and-gold red-soled heels.

" You look," Bastion stood with his mouth open and fangs fully extended. He couldn't finish the words. Autumn could see his fangs extending, along with his member, as she slowed her twirl to give a little over-the-shoulder wink.

"I looook…," Autumn teased Bastion a little more by doing a sexy little pose. She stared into his eyes as if she were the predator and he the prey.

"Good enough to eat you, my dear," Bastion finally said, gathering himself as he moved in close to taste his gorgeous angel. He moved so fast she didn't have to react.

"Bastion!" she yelped as he playfully kissed and nipped at her neck.

"Yes, my golden queen?" he said into her sweet-smelling neck. She smelled of not just her normal delicious aroma of honeysuckle and jasmine but this time … tonight she smelled of fiery confidence, sexiness, and glorious paradise. Tonight she would smell of him, as he planned to make her his … forever.

He clutched her as if she were going to disappear.

" Bastion, honey. You okay?" She asked, worried. He loosened his grip and held her out by her hands.

"Autumn, when I had this dress tailored for you, I wasn't confident it would be what I had envisioned to showcase your beauty, but I should have trusted Ms. Wang's thoughts and confidence more. ,The stars tonight will be dim in comparison to how brightly and beautifully you shine, my love. You look as beautiful as the ancient Nubian queens envisioned their future daughters." Autumn blushed hard. Her body was heating up and he started to feel her skin warm.

He laughed and kissed the top of her head. He didn't kiss her face, as he knew she wanted to keep her makeup neat. He thought about that and laughed to himself. "It's okay for now, tonight all that makeup will be sweated off. Before we leave for the gala, I wanted to give you something." Bastion announced.

"Honey, you've already done so much for me. I love being here and spending time with you. Honestly, double dating with the conjoined twins Royce and Sasha has been kind of fun." Autumn had to admit that she was really enjoying being with someone. It had been a very long time, and she needed to feel love and be loved again.

Bastion cupped her hands and kissed them gently. "My sweet Nubian queen. You deserve to sparkle tonight and every night, forever. I want to make sure you always do, if you'll allow me." He turned her toward the tall mirror and gave her two-carat black diamond earrings to go with the yellow and black diamond choker and bracelet she already wore. Autumn's mouth hung wide open.

"Bastion!" she whispered. "They're beautiful!"

Bastion's eyes began to change to the icy blue hue she loved and lusted after. He was everything she ever wanted and hadn't realized she needed. As she finished putting the chandelier earrings on, she admired them in the mirror. Bastion bent slightly, then started nipping and kissing the back of her neck as he stood behind her. His eyes had turned that hypnotizing blue shade again, and she felt her body temp increase as she fell into a lustful trance.

"You guys done ruining your clothes and ready to leave? The car is out front!" Sasha's giggly voice could be heard from outside the bedroom door.

"We're on our way," Autumn called back toward the door. Bastion gave her a sneaky half smile, slipped his hand into the slit of her dress, and started to play with her pussy.

"We are ready indeed. To go to the gala? Maybe in about an hour or so," Bastion said as he kissed her.

Autumn laughed as she kissed him and pulled his hand from her soaked panties. "Honey, you promised the stars, remember? We have to go or it will be morning when we come back up for air."

Bastion finally complied and laughed a little. "Baby girl, I don't need air," he said as he winked and sucked her juices from his fingers.

"We're coming out now," Autumn called to Sasha and Royce as she opened the door to their room.

Bastion smiled and whispered to her as they walked closer to the front entrance. "Not yet, but we will."

Autumn blushed as colorfully as a southern peach as she got to Sasha.

"Hey, you look gorgeous!" Sasha said, hugging her best friend.

"Oh, thanks boo. So do you!" Sasha wore a long, hunter-green form-fitting Versace dress that was cut low in the front and tied around the neck. Her hair fell in a waterfall of dark brown curls. "You smell like sex and roses," Autumn murmured with a side eye to Sasha, who looked straight ahead as they got comfortable in the custom Bentley.

"Excuse, ma'am, please mind your business. Thanks," Sasha said, smiling slightly.

Autumn smiled at her friend and watched the passing lights as the four rode through the snow-covered streets of Switzerland to the Star Diamond Light Gala at the new observatory.

"Ooooo, Bitch! This is so bougie! I love it!" Sasha said, still looking at the entrance of the event.

"Ma'am, may I help you out the car?"

The valet had reached inside the car and Royce defensively said, "Nah man, I got her. Thanks." The valet bowed and acknowledged the request, and Royce jumped out the car, moving quickly around the car to grab Sasha's hand. She shot Royce a sexy, surprised look and spread her legs slightly as she got out the car. Royce had to bite his lip as he reached for her and helped her stand. "Girl, you betta stop with all that spicy sauce. You gone fool around and get ate up in here," he whispered just low enough for her, Autumn, and Bastion to hear.

Autumn and Bastion cleared their throats and giggled a little as the horny pair walked into the event.

Autumn gathered her purse and, as she turning toward the door to step out, Bastion's hand reached for hers. She was stunning. Her golden skin magnified against the night sky and he was even more entranced by her. She seemed to emit her own light and heat as she emerged from the car to stand in front of him. "My God, love. You are just everything."

"Thank you, Bastion." She blushed as he helped her step closer to him. As they walked toward the entrance, he could feel the heat from her and felt himself getting aroused. *This will be a magical night to forever remember This is just the beginning of our forever,* Bastion thought. He glanced at her and smiled as he felt her hold him close to her as they walked in.

*   *   *

"Good evening, Ms. Catherine. Your escort to the gala has arrived," her butler said, waiting for her next command. Catherine was admiring herself in her floor-to-ceiling mirror one last time before she made an appearance at the event.

"Yes, tell him I'll be down in moment."

"As you wish, ma'am," her butler rushed away.

Goddamn, Catherine. You are fucking sexy, she told herself as she turned to see the most perfect ass and hips money could buy. She wore a skin-tight, white, strapless Christen Dior bandage mini dress that would cause traffic to stop and instant heart attacks.

Her makeup was flawless and made her pale skin look like untouched porcelain. She had her hair pulled into a slick, long blond ponytail. Her look was topped off with fire-red five-inch Balenciaga heels to match her Urban Decay DOA red lipstick. She smiled a horribly evil smile and thought, *Tonight Sebastion, you will know who you are truly supposed to belong to.* Her fangs extended and she smiled once more as she applied her clear gloss, grabbed her tiny clutch, and walked out of her bedroom.

As she walked toward her front door and to the black Rolls Royce, she thought about how delicious her victory over Sebastion would be. Her fangs extended again. She could almost taste the blood of his rage and she loved it. "See you soon, my angry pet," she purred. The door to the car closed and she was on her way. As she rode through the city, she thought of the many ways she was going to make Sebastion suffer. Ever since she saw him happy with that mortal bitch, her blood had boiled. *I still don't understand why she's so fucking special. Whatever. I don't care, nor am I concerned. What's a goon to a goblin?"* Catherine laughed to herself as she touched up her gloss again.

"Good evening Ms. May I assist you?" The valet opened the door and reached his hand in to the car.

"Yes, you may." She grabbed the valet's hand and was assisted out of the car. She stood a towering six foot three inches tall and looked like an evil Amazonian warrior. She was mesmerizing, but had a dark and twisted look in her eyes, one of possession, ownership, and confident privilege.

"Will anyone be joining you, Ms?"

Catherine rolled her eyes at the question. "No. I will be leaving with someone, though."

"Very good ma'am. We will escort you inside to the event.

As any gala would be, it was filled with beautiful and rich people from around the world. There was a lot of money in this room, and it felt different. It felt like they were supposed to be there. Autumn and Sasha mingled with royalty, old and new money, and nobody knew they were just regular people from Saint Louis. Bastion and Royce chatted up old pals and new business associates. Mira had shown up later in the evening with her Greek god of a man. She met up with her brothers as they moved among the crowd.

"Hey, Mira!" Royce hugged his sister.

"Hey fellas, sorry I'm late. I was … busy, you know."

"Yes!" Royce exclaimed. "Maybe now you'll finally relax."

Mira rolled her eyes.

"Hey, big sis," Bastion hugged Mira.

"So when does the show start?" she asked. "I hope it's soon."

"Yeah, I'd say in the next 30 minutes or so. I'll go check," Bastion offered.

Bastion hurried off, and Autumn and Sasha finally returned to the group.

"Ooooo, hey gorgeous where have you been all my life?" Royce said, pulling Sasha close.

", Royce, you're so, .umm," Sasha said as she rubbed her booty up against him as he hugged her from behind.

Autumn and Mira looked at the two. "Yuck you guys. Get a room."

Autumn smiled, then asked, "Where's Bastion?"

"Oh, he went to see when the show is supposed to start. He'll be right back," Mira answered as her gentleman walked up to her.

"Okay," Autumn said, feeling lonely as the two couples were starting to boo up. "I think I'll go look for him," she added, excusing herself from the group. As she walked through the crowd she saw him looking visibly upset. He was talking to a tall, pale woman. She was incredibly beautiful, almost too beautiful to be real. She stood close to him with her hand on his chest and looked like she was trying to talk him into something.

Who the fuck is that? Autumn wondered. *I should go over there and introduce myself. Nah, that's petty. It's all good, I'll let it be."* Autumn could feel her blood pressure rise, as well as her body temperature. She could feel the anger in her rise, as this woman seemed to be angering Bastion. She finally turned away and walked back to where she had left the group. The look on her face signaled her anger. Sasha noticed, immediately came out of her Royce-induced trance. "Bitch, what's wrong?" Sasha asked, feeling upset for her friend.

"Nothing. I'm going to go to the restroom," Autumn said, and Sasha followed right behind her.

Mira looked concerned. "Royce! What just happened?"

Royce glanced around, confused, and finally zeroed in on Bastion. "Oh shit!" he said, nodding toward Bastion.

"What?" Mira struggled to see over everyone. "What's wrong?"

Royce grabbed Mira's hand and pulled her just out of earshot of Bastion and Catherine.

"Oh shit!" Mira said.

"This isn't good at all. Not at all," Royce said as he moved quickly toward Bastion and Catherine. As Royce got closer, he could hear the two arguing.

"Sebastion, why do you keep denying the fact that we are meant to be together? You're wasting your time on a stupid, fucking mortal. And for what? Because she looks exotic? Because she's black? Sebastion, Let's be honest. You're just going to fuck her and once you get bored you'll be back to me."

Bastion hated her so much. "Catherine, get your hands off me."

She backed up a little, a horribly satisfied fanged smile on her face. "Come on, Sebastion! She'll never be me! You know this, yet you continue to piss me off by playing these stupid fucking games!" She was starting to get loud and was beginning to draw the attention of others.

"Whoa, whoa!" Royce ran up to intervene before a fight began, standing between Bastion and Catherine. "Bastion, go find Autumn and the rest of the group and let's go find our seats."

"Aw, you brought your little mortal bitch with you? How fucking touching," Catherine spat in the ground.

"Get the fuck out of here, Catherine," Bastion said, slowly losing his cool. His eyes began to turn black and Royce was struggling to keep Bastion from mauling her.

"Catherine! Get the fuck out of here like he said!" Royce said.

"Fine," Catherine said, claws engaged and fangs fully extended. "Just remember, Bastion, you can't keep her hidden forever. When I find her, she'll die."

"Stay the fuck away from her, Catherine!" Bastion roared.

"Bastion! Chill, bro!" Royce was trying to hold him away from her. Mira ran up after Catherine scurried away, laughing.

"Bastion! Look at me!" Mira said. She held her brother's rage infused face. " Bastion, relax. You need to go find Autumn, right now. She came looking for you, and I think she saw you and Catherine arguing."

Bastion realized what Mira was saying. "Fuck! Where'd she go?"

"She went to the restroom with Sasha," Mira responded. Bastion hugged Mira and hurried off to find Autumn.

"Alright girl, what happened?" Sasha asked, consoling her friend.

"I don't know. I went to go find Bastion and I did, but something was wrong," Autumn said as she sat on the little sofa in the restroom.

"What does that mean?" Sasha seemed frustrated.

Autumn, feeling upset, sad, angry, and let down, wanted to cry. "He was talking to some really tall, pale chick. Not like he was trying to get at her or anything but like he was really upset or something. Like he used to mess with her and she tried to get him or something." Sasha finally sat next to her.

"Ughhh, yeah." Autumn said as she sighed. "Oh wow."

"Damn, hun. What do you want to do? You know I'm here for you, ride or die," Sasha assured her best friend.

"Thanks, love. Give me a few minutes and I'll be out," Autumn said.

"Okay, well I'll wait outside and let Royce and Mira know we'll meet them at our seats if you still want to stay. It's whatever you want to do."

Autumn smiled. "Okay. Love you."

"Love you too, bitch," Sasha hugged her friend and walked out.

Outside the restroom, Bastion hurried up to her. "Listen, Bastion. I don't know what kind of game you are playing, but don't mess with my friend," Sasha said as soon as she saw him.

Bastion saw how upset Sasha was and hurriedly explained what happened. "Sasha, I love Autumn, I want to tell her, and I will, but right now I have to explain to her what I just explained to you."

Sasha, still looking concerned, said, "Well, you fucking better. Get in there."

As Bastion stepped into the women's restroom, the other women looked shocked. "I know ladies. Thanks," he said to the room.

"Autumn? May I come talk to you?" Bastion asked.

"Sure," Autumn said as she returned to the small sofa.

Bastion sat next to her.

"We don't fit on this couch," she said, annoyed.

"I'll sit on the floor," Bastion replied, then sat on the restroom floor cross-legged, his hands in his chin and waited for her to look at him.

"Bastion! Get up! This floor is dirty!"

"Nope," he said. "Not until you hear me out."

" Ugh. Fine! Okay!"

Bastion smiled like a little kid and began to explain what and who Autumn saw. She was right about her being an ex, but she couldn't explain the instant rage she felt in her body. It was a feeling she had never had before, like an ancient rage boiling just beneath the surface, ready to burst out and burn everything and everyone to ash.

"Autumn, my love. You mean so much to me. Our thirty days are almost up, and I want you to know I was very serious about this just being the beginning." Bastion held up her chin to look into her eyes. "Autumn, say something, love." He was on edge with worry. Everything had gone beautifully for the past twenty-eight days. This week was leading up to a truly special night, and then worst thing that could possibly happen—Catherine Ortega—had happened.

"Bastion, I have enjoyed these last few days, as they have been some of the most incredible of my life. You've made me feel so happy and, better yet, safe. I feel like another side of myself is exposed around you, and only you bring it out of me."

"Will you allow me to continue to show you why you mean so much to me tonight?" he asked, feeling like his heart would explode.

She looked at him with unsure, questioning eyes.

"Come on, gorgeous. Let me show you off to the stars and make them jealous for how you shine."

Autumn smiled a little at him, as his eyes were starting to turn ice blue. "Is that a yes?"

Autumn giggled, as this grown man was sitting on the floor, cross-legged in a Balenciaga suit, asking her to be with him.

"Please, Autumn?" he said again.

" Fine," she said with a quiet smile.

"What was that?" he asked, smiling a little closer to her face.

"Yes!" she said louder and laughed.

"Yes!" he replied as he kissed her before she could object. "Now, let's get out of here before security gets called on me.""Let's," she agreed as he helped her up and into his arms.

As they walked into the observatory, Bastion whispered, "I'm so very grateful you decided to join me tonight."

Autumn started to blush and felt her body start to heat up. "Thank you for inviting me and for everything so far."

"You liked the gifts, then? Everything you've experienced has been good?" Bastion wanted to make sure he was on the right path to her heart.

"Yes, Bastion." She hugged his arm as they found their seats with Royce, Sasha, Mira, and her escort. "Everything is perfect."

He could feel her soft glow, and her scent teased his senses. "Shall we sit? They're getting ready for the unveiling."

"Yes, let's!" she said. That did it for Bastion. He was in love. She squeezed his arm in antici-pation, and it felt perfect.

As everyone took their seats, Catherine's hawk eyes zeroed in on Sebastion's part, particu-larly him and the mortal.

Fuck! she thought. *Disgusting.* Then her thoughts turned to how she would make him suffer. *Soon, Sebastion. Very soon.*

As she was deep in her toxic thoughts, a loud voice was heard. "Ladies and gentlemen. Thank you for joining us for the first Star Diamond Light Gala. Tonight, we will be viewing the galaxies up close and as clear as 4K TV through the world's most powerful telescope."

"The speech takes all the fun out of stargazing, huh?" Bastion whispered to Autumn.

She giggled and playfully punched him "Bastion!. Behave, sir."

He laughed softly and kissed her hair. It was solidified. He absolutely loved her.

As the speech ended, the workers opened the ceiling to reveal the clearest and darkest skies they had ever seen. "Ohhh! Wow!" She whispered, her mouth as wide as her eyes. "There are so many constellations and so little time." Autumn had turned into a little kid looking up at the stars. She was so excited and happy and she had to stop and think to really grasp that she was so in love.

Bastion loved how her face legitimately lit up and had such a soft, pinkish-gold glow. She was so innocently beautiful.

She leaned over to him and whispered, "Bastion, this is the best date ever!" Then she kissed him hard on the cheek.

His heart nearly leaped out of his chest. His heart, which really hasn't beated in 600 years. He was cool about feeling like a schoolboy, though. "Anything I can do to make you smile forever, my love, I will do."

Autumn smiled. "Okay, well, I need to get something to drink and to freshen up."

Bastion's smile glowed in the dimly lit ballroom as he held her hand, helping her stand from her seat.

"Okay, let me escort you, my love." As they moved through the crowd, they were being followed. Once they were away from the crowded ballroom, Autumn turned around and kissed him.

Bastion was a little shocked, but embraced her fully. He loved the taste of her. Finally coming up for air he said, "What was that for and how do I get more of it?"

She blushed and said into his chest, "You're amazing, Sebastion. I don't know the words to describe what I'm feeling right now, but I know you sparked something. You awaked something inside me. I feel it stir up in me every time we collide."

Bastion's mouth fell open a little because he wasn't sure how she felt, but her words hit him.

"I wanted to get to know you when I first met you in my store. I was kind of shy and wasn't sure you saw me as someone you'd want to spend time with."

"I felt the same way!" she said. "I was really nervous and it felt awkward because I really liked you."

Bastion grabbed her waist and brought her closer to him. She was so small and perfect. "I saw you then and see you now." Bastion was on cloud nine. They both were, and nobody on earth mattered right now. "I want you in all ways, Autumn." She kissed him softly and said, "Let me go, honey, and you can tell me more of what you have in mind." She gave him a sexy look over her shoulder and winked at him as she walked into the restroom.

Bastion hesitantly let her go, watching her walk into the restroom. His eyes were ice blue, his fangs slightly extended as he waited for his beautiful Nubian queen.

"Damn, excuse me," Autumn said as a pale, tall, blond woman bumped into her as she walked passed. Catherine snarled and said, "Disgusting human bitch."

Autumn, who was washing her hands, turned to Catherine and politely said, "Excuse me? What did you say?"

Catherine smiled her evil, happy smile and walked up to Autumn, claws full out and fangs fully extended, to repeat what she said. "You heard me right, you stupid, useless, mortal trash. All your kind is good for is food and fucking." Catherine pushed Autumn hard into the back wall.

Something in Autumn broke free. Her eyes flashed and turned molten gold, she grew her own talons, and her body ignited into a walking flame.

Catherine was amazed and slightly terrified, but that didn't stop her jumping to attack her.

She threw one punch to her face and Autumn fell. Catherine leaned over her and moved to slash her throat.

Autumn's eyes flew open and she grabbed Catherine by the throat and threw her across the bathroom into the mirrors.

Catherine wasn't prepared for so much power to come out of one mortal person. "What are you?" Catherine screamed as she bled and moved to attack Autumn again. "I'm that bitch who's not to be fucked with period!" As more fire burned and glass shattered, the rest of the party was roaring.

Outside of the restroom, Bastion was patiently waiting when two bigger vampires walked up to him. "What's up, fellas?" he asked in a relaxed manner.

"Mr. Roberston, you need to come with us now," one of the fat vampires said.

Bastion wasn't down with people telling him what he needed to do. "Nah, I'm cool," he said as his eyes turned black and his fangs extended in attack mode.

"That wasn't a request, bitch," the second vampire said.

"Fuck you! What the fuck you want, huh?" Bastion demanded.

Suddenly, blood and fire erupted from the ladies room.

"Get your fucking hands off me, you crazy fire bitch!" a woman screamed.

"I'll fucking show you crazy, you pale-ass psychopath! You thought you could insult me and put your hands on me and I wouldn't defend myself!"

Catherine, despite being burned and bloody was still full of fight. The women had fought their way out of the ladies room and were now in the middle of the gala.

" So, who just invites mortals, let alone black ones, to these events anyway?" Autumn became even more infuriated and punched Catherine through a glass barrier.

"Shut up, you useless pile of dead skin!" Autumn shouted as she glowed red-hot. Catherine laughed as her mouth bled and picked herself up off the floor.

As the women fought in the middle of the event, the various creatures of the lore were spellbound. Bastion and the fat vampires, as well as everyone else, were in awe that the legend of the Race of the Phoenix was true. They had fused their DNA with mortals for concealment and survival.

Sasha could see her friend in flames, but not burning. It was like she was the flame. Sasha was speechless.

Royce, ready to fight, finally found Bastion and asked if he had a problem. "Nah bro, I'm good. I don't think Catherine will be, though."

Royce looked confused, then he realized who the women fighting were.

"Bro! What the fuck! Autumn's a real phoenix?"

Catherine had now morphed into a hideous demon beast and was giving Autumn a run for her money. They continued to fight, as Autumn's flame and power began to change. Her talons grew longer and became blades of black obsidian. She grew wings of fire, using them as a shield against Catherine's claws, which were now dripping poison.

" Listen, mortal!" Catherine growled and jumped on top of Autumn.

"Get the fuck off me, you nasty-ass demon bitch!"

"Or what, you whatever you are. I'll crush your tiny neck and nobody can save you," Catherine snarled, then began to squeeze her neck. Autumn's eyes flashed liquid silver and she let a sonic screech. Catherine screamed and covered her ear holes. Everyone else covered their ears and took cover as the glass throughout the building shattered. Autumn's screech took her flame to another level of heat, which began to burn Catherine's skin.

Catherine, realizing she was burning, jumped off of Autumn, who jumped to her feet and ran toward Catherine, raining blow after blow of fire onto the demonic woman.

Catherine's skin began to melt and finally fell to the floor. The room fell silent as Catherine screamed, "What is happening to my skin?"

Finally, her bodyguards picked her up and carried her quickly out of the building. Autumn stood there in her full on firebird glory, still a flame as she watched Catherine's burned-up body being carried away. Once Catherine and her bodyguards were out of sight, Autumn's flame form disappeared and she fainted, falling to the floor.

Bastion rushed to her. "Autumn! Autumn!" He yelled. "Mira! Royce! Get a medic now!" The two raced away to find a medic.

Catherine, in the meantime, was rushed to her house and up to her room. The family's senior butler was called to attend her.

"Call her brother and the hospital now," he ordered quickly.

Catherine's house was in a frenzy. Still dazed, Catherine laughed, thinking she would heal but that fire bitch would be dead from her poison. As Catherine's burned body lay there, she thought about how strong Autumn was. *How could a fucking mortal channel so much ancient power?* "What the fuck!" she screamed. Her staff was terrified of her, but she had taken a real beating and they were even more terrified of what did that to her.

As Autumn lay unresponsive on the observatory floor, Bastion could feel her energy still stirring. It wasn't finished. Suddenly, Autumn's body ignited again and her eyes flew open. She wasn't herself anymore.

"Autumn, can you hear me?" Bastion stared into her golden eyes and heard the whispered screech of a wounded bird. Her wings appeared, and as she sat up, looking into Bastion's concerned face. Her now-golden talons flexed as she stood, spread her wings, and flew away. Bastion saw his firebird's light streaking across the sky. "Autumn!" Bastion screamed after her.

"I have to find her!" Bastion roared as Mira and Royce returned with the only doctor they could find at the gala. The two looked frantically at their brother, then looked at the doctor, who was an elder elf.

"What do we do?" Mira whispered. Bastion was on his knees, begging the doctor for help.

"The lore behind the phoenix race is that once they reach their full form they will burn them-selves to be born anew," the doctor spoke quickly. "This means she will go somewhere secluded and hard to find."

He turned to Bastion. "Was she responsive to your voice? If she was, she is still able to be saved. If not, she will burn herself to death to regenerate. Once she regenerates, she will no longer remember this life, her past life. She will have flashes of her past, but it will seem like a watered-down dream."

Bastion wasn't about to lose his dream, his fantasy, his world, his forever love.

Sasha grabbed Royce, tears in her eyes from losing Autumn. "Royce! What the fuck! Where's Autumn? Y'all crazy up in here!"

"Sasha, baby. I don't know what just happened, but we will find her." Royce wrapped his arms around her, holding a screaming Sasha into his chest to console her.

"Doc, what do we need to do? How do we help her?" Bastion was freaking out, but the doc-tor was thinking hard.

"Where was the last place she was really and truly comfortable? A place she felt safe and loved?"

Bastion thought of this week and everything that led up to this point.

She was happiest at the Chalet! he realized.

Bastion jumped up and ran toward the front entrance of the building, where the rest of the other gala attendees had been evacuated from the building. That didn't stop them, of course, from Instagramming, Snapchatting, FaceBooking, or Tweeting out footage of a real phoenix rising.

The valet staff, fire department, police, and a massive number of spectators were all around. Bastion found a Maserati and its keys near the valet stand and took off toward the chalet.

She's got to be there, he thought desperately. Bastion was sweating bullets, wondering if she'd gone back to her normal state and lay lying dying somewhere in the house. Or worse, she'd flown to some distant mountain to burn herself to death, only to return remembering nothing of who she was.

"Oh, gods, please let her be here!" he cried out as he got close to the chalet and could see it was still as dark as they had left it.

He skidded the car to a stop at the front door and ran inside, leaving the door hanging open behind him.

"Autumn!" he yelled, over and over again as he ran through the house and the back garden area through the snow and into the darkness, screaming her name. Nothing. *She's not here.*

His mind scrambled for another possibility, and he ran back in the house. He was distraught. Falling to his knees, his hands out stretched to the sky, all he could do was moan and call out her name. Royce, Mira, Sasha, and Mateo, Mira's gentleman companion, rushed into the house to find Bastion on his knees, bloody tears streaming down his face.

"Oh, God, no!" Sasha cried. "Bastion! She's not here?" Sasha broke down, and Royce grabbed her to keep her from collapsing.

Mira dropped to her knees in front of Sebastion and hugged her brother. "Sebastion, she's not dead yet. The doctor said she's got somewhere safe and where she felt at home. Listen little brother, what if she flew all the way home? To Saint Louis?"

Bastion raised his blood-stained face and looked puzzled, then hopefully at his big sister. "Oh my God, Mira, you're a genius. I have to get back to Saint Louis now!"

Royce was already on his cell phone. "I'm on the phone with Quinton now. He said Jones has already contacted air traffic control to let them know you'll be taking the quickest flight back to the States. The jet is being prepped and fueled as we speak." As he coordinated with the staff, Royce held Sasha as if he never wanted to risk losing her again.

"Bastion, once you find her, you'll have to teach her. Help her understand who and what she is, but more importantly, you'll have to love her. She's extremely vulnerable, so please be careful," Mira said as her brother rushed to get himself together for his flight.

"I swear. That's only if she'll forgive and still have me," Bastion promised. He was getting emotional again. *How could I have failed to protect her?*

"Mira, what if she dies?" he whispered.

"Stop it, Bastion! She's a fucking phoenix for the lore's sake. Her bloodline is older them most things in the lore and I'm confident her inner fire won't allow her to die."

Bastion loved his sister's optimism. She wiped his face and helped him get his shit together so he could leave.

Royce continued to coordinate so Bastion could have the smoothest and fastest ways back to Saint Louis possible. He arranged for a car to take him from the chalet, with a police escort to get him to the airport with no stops. "Looks like you were right about Autumn being a rarity," Royce said, leaning in Bastin's doorway and watching he and Mira pack. "Everything's good to go." Bastion looked up and at his brother. He'd always been a joker, but he looked more concerned and sincere about how he was feeling. He didn't say it, but he felt it."

Bastion rose, walked over to his brother, and hugged him. They loved each other, but this hug was filled with unspoken words of encouragement and understanding. No words were needed because it was understood.

"Mr. Robertson, sir, your transport has arrived," Quinton said.

"Very good, Quinton. Thank you." Bastion grabbed his bags, hugged his siblings, and turned to Sasha.

"Bastion! Wait! Please tell her that I'll see her soon and that she is loved." Sasha looked sad and scared. "Please find her," she added.

Bastion smiled at them and promised, "I'll die before I let go. I promise to find her."

He stepped into the car and it was a mad dash to the airport and the plane.

"Where to, Mr. Robertson?" the pilot asked.

"Home, please. I have to find my forever." The pilot nodded and cleared the tower for take-off. "Please to all the gods in the universe," Bastion prayed. "Let her still be alive."

*   *   *

As Bastion was flying back to Saint Louis, Autumn the firebird was tucked away in the one place she felt safe. Her mythical form had brought her back to her nest and once she was finally settled into her own space surrounded by her things, the phoenix form finally let her go. Her clothes had burned all the way, and the little bit of energy the phoenix form could muster allowed her to fall into her bed.

Autumn was in a coma-like sleep, and everything that had transpired was just an crazy dream she could wake up from.

"What the hell?" Autumn woke from her sleep. "Uggggghhh, damn I'm sore." " What happened?" she repeated. "I must have been in a car accident or something. I'm covered in bruises and dried blood. Is it mine? I don't see any cuts. And I stink and need a fucking shower." Autumn struggled to get out of her bed and limp past her mirror. "Damn. Would've been nice if someone told me I looked like shit after a car accident." Autumn was still examining all the bruises. "I'll call Sasha's ass later," she decided. She started the bath water and poured in some Epsom salt and lavender as she tried to remember what happened. *Nothing! Damn it. Let me soak and just relax.* Autumn told herself as she climbed into the tub. *Shit, if I look this bad … I wonder what the person feels like?****

"Why the fuck am I not healing faster? This shit really fucking hurts!!" Catherine was screaming at her resident witch doctor.

"Please Ms. Catherine. Your burns aren't like regular burns. Whatever attacked you is ancient."

"So? What does that have to do with my wounds not healing faster?" Catherine was a terrible patient. No wasn't a word she was used to, and she'd been hearing it a lot lately. "Damn it! What do I pay you for?"

The witch doctor looked at Catherine and politely said, " Ms, first of all, your brother pays me to care for you. Second, when I say ancient I mean mythical ancient. I'm not absolutely sure, but if I were a gambling woman, I'd say you were attacked by a Phoenix."

Catherine rolled over on her side so the doctor could bandage her and said, "What do you mean a phoenix? If they even existed, they'd be from the God Realm, wouldn't they?" Catherine rolled her eyes as she cringed while getting stitched up. "Ouch! You stupid … grrrr!!!" Behind Catherine's closed eyelids, all she could see was Autumn turning into a great firebird and igniting. That was the last thing she remembered.

Not possible, she thought. "Sebastion just happened to be dating a fucking phoenix. They have been gone for millennia.

Catherine was deep in her own thought when they were interrupted by her brother's voice. "What happened, Catherine? Were you ambushed?"

Zepher was very defensive of his baby sister and wanted nothing but to see her happy. He had flown halfway around the world to see if the news was true and if his sister was really involved.

Catherine was slightly embarrassed, but she held her chin up as if she had just lost their first title fight.

"Hello brother," Catherine growled over the last bit of stitch her witch doctor was putting in her newly grafted skin in an attempt to her melted face.

"What in the old and new worlds did this to you? And why aren't you healing as fast as you should be?" Zepher was both frustrated and fascinated with this.

"You're extremely lucky, Catherine," the witch doctor said as she was cleaning up and greeting her brother.

Zepher took a seat next to Catherine's bed. "So, what happened, since I definitely told you not to go to this gala and to let Sabastion be with his miserable human."

Catherine rolled her eyes as if she were being lectured and decided to keep the exact nature of her injuries to herself.

"Listen, Zepher, I do what I want because I'm grown. That means I'll let him go when I decide to let him go." Zepher held the bridge of his nose as if his was talking to a living headache. Catherine was indeed that, and not just for him, obviously.

"I will tell you that his little human is no average human," she said, patting her bandages because they were starting to itch from healing.

"What does that even mean? You mean to tell me you go into fight with

a human and she did this to you?" Zepher wanted to laugh, but didn't so he could hear this explanation. Catherine was getting upset and began to get flustered. "First of all, I said she wasn't some average bitch and, as you can see, I'm not alright with it." Zepher couldn't hold his smile back and giggled a little. "Get out, Zepher. You aren't any help and I don't need your carelessness, thanks." Catherine turned over as if she was going to get some sleep.

"Okay, Cat. If she isn't an average human, then what could she possibly be to do this kind of damage to an older vampire?"

Catherine, however, was done talking to Zepher. "Goodnight, Zepher." Zepher let out a sigh and stood, kissed her head, and walked out of her room.

As he walked toward the front door, he was greeted by the witch doctor. "Ingrid, what really happened to Catherine?" Zepher asked as they walked out of the house.

"Zepher, your sister is a real piece of work and I'll be asking for a raise dealing with her from now on."

Zepher rolled his eyes. " Fine, now what happened to her?"

Ingrid was packing up her car and turned to Zepher with her arms crossed. "She was attacked by a phoenix."

Zepher's eyes were wide and he burst out laughing. No way. That's not possible."

Ingrid looked unamused and tired of explaining the diagnosis. "Listen, I'm pretty sure I'm the only professional here, but what the fuck do I know." she got in her car and said to Zepher, " I'll be back tomorrow to check on her and change her bandages, but you need to warn her to stay away from that phoenix."

Zepher was looking less amused this time when she said it.

" Wait, you're serious? A no-shit phoenix attacked Catherine?"

Ingrid looked at Zepher, still tired of explaining, and said, " Yes, I'll be back tomorrow." Ingrid got in her car and left. Zepher was left in Catherine's driveway as she sped away. He thought a minute to digest what Ingrid and Catherine were saying. *That's not possible though. A phoenix, here? They've been extinct for millennium. Oh shit, maybe the legends about them splicing their DNA with humans aren't just legends?* Zepher was everywhere on this.

While Zepher was trying to wrap his mind around Catherine being attacked by a phoenix, Catherine was still seething with rage. "You're extremely lucky," She remembered Ingrid saying.

Catherine turned her burned face behind her bandages. " We'll see how lucky that bitch is once I'm healed. Next time I see her, I'm snapping her neck on sight." Catherine was finally feeling the effects of the sleep medication Ingrid gave her and drifted off to sleep.

*   *   *

"Autumn is a what?" Mira couldn't believe what she was hearing. "Hold on." She had to sit down. "Didn't they die out or just evolve into something else?" Mira was trying to wrap her mind around the notion that Dr. Autumn Scorpeno, the lead doctor in her hospital as well as in her field of medicine, is a legitimate mythical phoenix goddess. "How do you know this,

Bastion?" Mira's mouth was left wide open as she FaceTimed with Bastion as he flew toward Saint Louis.

Bastion took a deep breath and began to explain about the explosion, blood, and flames that happened at the gala and what he saw that night. Bastion wasn't about to explain his extremely wet and inappropitate dream that gave him his first clue. That wasn't for anyone's ears.

"Wooow!" is all Mira could muster in reply.

"I've been doing some research, and I found some really old Egyptian lore. I had to contact my boys to get the scrolls scanned to me." Royce was now in frame and he and Mira were both intrigued. Bastion began to explain, Phoenix gods are supposed to live up 1500 years before they die, but they don't ever actually die. They set themselves on fire and burn to ashes and nothingness. However, during that period of incineration, their life energy is transferred to the universe and transcends the galaxies till it reemerges in a worthy being. That being is a stronger force, as the phoenix is now reborn to live again."

"This is fucking wild!" Royce yelled in excitement.

"Okay, so Autumn is an immortal goddess but doesn't know it?" Mira asked, just as excited.

"Yeah, basically," Bastion said, fascinated. "Well, Shit bro, guess we will be on our way to help you find your goddess," Mira said, ready for some action.

"Thank you guys," Bastion said "See you soon."

*   *   *

"Autumn … hun …. talk to me. What's been going on?" Sasha practically begged her friend. Sasha had flown back to St. Louis before Royce and Mira because of the incident at the gala. Being the Special Agent in charge of the DEA's Saint Louis field office had its perks, but it was also very demanding. Sasha had stayed busy trying to run a few background checks on who would attack Autumn and why. But the investigation was going nowhere fast, so being a friend to Autumn now was the next best thing to help her friend.

" Nothing, I'm fine. It's just been a long couple of weeks. Working and such." Since the incident in Switzerland, Autumn has been a hermit, coming and going only to the grocery store and work. She passed the bookstore on her way to and from work, and every time the magic of it pulled at her emotions and caused her skin to heat.

Autumn was still upset about how her magical trip ended in her being medically transferred home. The worst part was that she had no idea what happened and Bastion was nowhere to be found. She felt dumb, stupid, and foolish. It wasn't that Bastion hadn't tried to contact her. He had tried to call, text, and FaceTime her several times a day, but she didn't want to answer. *Why should I answer? You aren't here to explain things to my face, so why should I entertain you at all?* She was getting upset. She felt that she had been played for a fool.

"Well, you want some company for dinner tonight? You know I hate cooking, but I will if it will get you to open your door."

Autumn cracked a smile on FaceTime with Sasha. "Thanks, love. I greatly appreciate it, but I'd rather just chill by myself."

Sasha was a little sad, but she understood. "Alright, hun, well, take a shower and put some less hobo looking clothes on. I'll FacetTime you later."

Autumn smiled and said, "Yes, ma'am. I'll even do my hair some kind of way. "

"Thanks, boo. Ttyl." Sasha blew her a kiss and hung up.

Autumn took a look at herself in the mirror and saw her bruises and scars were healing more and more each day. She could still feel the emotional and mental pain, but she was making it through each day. *I guess I could spruce myself up a little and not be a hermit*, she decided.

Sasha looked at the selfies she and Autumn had taken the week of the gala and she smiled. *What happened to this beautiful person?* Sasha was feeling sad when her phone rang again.

"Hello?"

"Well hello gorgeous. It's Royce," A sultry baritone voice sounded through the phone.

"Oh, wow, really? How can I help you, sir?" Sasha was surprised and pissed.

"Well, damn, that wasn't very warm, love. I'm sorry I haven't reached out since our adventure, but I need your help."

Sasha looked at her phone then rolled her eyes. "First of all," Sasha was about to go in on Royce with all the Afro Latina spice. "Our adventures were whatever …"

Royce's mouth flew open in offense. "They were … whatever?"

"Yep, but I'm not tripping about that. What does piss me off is how your brother thought he could play my friend to the left."

Royce was getting upset. "Hold on, hold on. What do you think happened, hun?" Royce was sounding defensive.

"She told me that she got into it with that white bitch for whatever she said to her about Bastion." Sasha was not up for listening to what Royce was trying to explain.

"Listen, Sasha, everything Catherine tried to do or say is because she's legit crazy and, for the record, Bastion had shit to do with any of that."

"Honestly, Royce, I'm not trying to hear any of this, but what can I help you with?"

Royce could sense the end of the conversation was rapidly approaching. "Sasha please. I'm trying to help Bastion get in touch with Autumn so he can explain what happened."

"Like I said Royce, I'm not trying to hear this, and I'm sure Autumn isn't either. If she wants to be found, she'll let him know. Till then adios." Sasha, not feeling sorry, hung up on Royce.

"Fuck!" Royce roared into the open space of his loft. "I hate that smart mouth of hers, but I love it!" Royce was in love with Sasha, but this wasn't the time for that. He needed to help his brother.

"Any luck from Sasha?" Bastion asked as he walked over to the couch with their drinks.

"Sasha isn't a fan of me right now, bro."

Bastion looked depressed. He got up and walked over to the floor-to-ceiling windows. "Royce, have I lost her?" Bastion asked his brother as he looked out unto the city skyline.

"Honestly, bro, I don't know. Everything that happened to her was life altering, and expecting she would easily come around to knowing or expecting to be alright with it is asking a tremendous amount from her."

"Strong women of color are definitely more complicated than I thought."

"Indeed. I love her so much and I need to tell her this and so much more," Bastion said to his brother.

"I know. We won't give up hope, we'll find her," Royce re-assured his brother." The fact that she's an ancient phoenix goddess and doesn't know it is a muuuch bigger issue."

Bastion took a deep breath and sighed. "Indeed."

"Have you been able to hack into her systems yet?" Catherine, fully recovered and meaner than ever, asked her specialized IT guy.

"Not yet Ms., I'm still working it," he said, staring into the screen.

"Well, hurry the fuck up! I need to know where she lives so we can finish this," She growled. Catherine was healed, but she hadn't really recovered. She still wore the scars from being beaten and even with her regenerative abilities she wasn't quite the same. Her hands and face had been specifically grafted from a donor she found. She was still super pissed about having to have surgery. That was bad, but the fact that it was due to some weird-ass black fire bitch made her even angrier. She could still feel how much it hurt in her face and hands. "Grrrrrr fuck!" she whispered.

"I found it Ms. Catherine! She lives in Saint Louis, Missouri, in the U.S. Here's her address."

"Good," she hissed. She had a calm, yet crazed look on her face. Catherine ran off to her room. As she began to pack her tactical bag, she had the most hideous thought. *I'm going to skin that bitch alive before I snap her neck.* She laughed to herself. *This is going to be fun.*

"Charles!" She yelled. "Ready the jet! We're going human hunting!"

"Very good, ma'am," Charles responded.

Catherine had finished her packing and was combat ready. She walked down to the foyer area to await her transport. As she was getting into her vehicle, the driver informed her, "Thirty minutes till wheels up, Ms. Catherine. It's a five hour flight to Saint Louis."

"Perfect" Catherine hissed as her fangs extended and her eyes turned black.

✦   ✦   ✦

Buzzzzz, buzzzz… Autumn opened one eye and groaned. "Hello?"

"Autumn. Please don't hang up. It's Sebastion."

Her eye popped wide open and her heart raced as she sat straight up in bed. *Stay calm and breathe,* she had to remind herself. "Hello Sebastion. How can I help you, sir?" Autumn wanted to scream at him. She wanted to be all the way up pissed at him. But she stayed as calm as she could given the hour of day it was.

"Autumn, I honestly don't know where to begin to apologize," Bastion began. "You deserve the stars and to be worshipped and I want to do all those things."

Autumn listened, but wasn't hearing what she needed to hear. "Sebastion, that's all well and good and you're right I do deserve all of those things. What is it that you want?" Autumn had to force herself to be strong. She was on the verge of tears and had to mute him so he wouldn't hear the shakiness in her voice.

"I'm calling to apologize and to beg your forgiveness."

"I don't know, Sebastion, you have a crazy ass white bitch who is clearly obsessed with you so much she'd kill someone over you. I just don't want that drama in my life," Autumn said confidently under her now-streaming tears.

She loved Sebastion and she wanted to tell him that. She had thought he felt the same way, but now she wasn't sure about anything.

"I know Autumn, please believe me when I say I don't give a fuck about her. She's a non-factor in my life and that's how it's always been." Autumn was quiet on the phone. " Are you still there? Autumn?" Bastion was beginning to panic.

"I'm still here." She had gotten up to get some tissues and was now sitting in her beanbag nest. "Why should I believe that, Sebastion?" She was getting upset. "She tried to kill me in the bathroom and if I hadn't blacked out I'm sure she would have."

Bastion paused. "Wait. Autumn, you don't remember what happened after that?"

Autumn was annoyed by the question. "Ugh. No, Sebastion. All I remember is she pushed me hard into the bathroom wall. The next thing I remember was waking up here in a burned-up dress covered in bruises."

Sebastion was slightly excited to know she didn't remember what happened, but even more terrified of telling her and exactly what she was. "Sebastion, honestly I really just …" Tears started to stream down her face, and her body heated from all of the emotions she felt. "I really liked you, but if I were to pursue a relationship with you then I'd constantly feel I was in danger." Sebastion was desperate not to lose her. "Autumn, please, give me a chance to explain everything. Let me come see you." Autumn's heart almost fell out of her chest. She missed him. This man was everything she ever wanted. It didn't matter he was white or a vampire or super tech savvy or shit even stupid rich. She had fallen for this man, only to be crushed by the weight of sadness from her last encounter with his life.

She wiped the hot tears from her face and stood her ground. "No, Sebastion. I'm not ready to see you in person. I'm still healing and I … just can't." Sebastion could feel the love of his life, his newly found destiny, his temple of fortitude, slipping away.

"Autumn, please let me explain everything and open myself up to you, completely."

Autumn was quiet again, contemplating if she should even allow a chance for any more hurt in her life.

"My love, are you still there?" Bastion was sweating bullets.

"Yes."

"Is that permission to come and see you then?"

Autumn sighed, then responded, "Sebsation, I have to take a bath if you're going to come by, and I don't want my house to be a wreck either. Be here in one hour."

"I will." Bastion's heart almost stopped again. She had agreed to see him. It seemed to have been forever since he had laid his eyes on her.

"Autumn, I swear you won't regret this. I swear."

"Fine. One hour Sebastion Robertson." Autumn hung up, and sat in her nest and thought for a second. *I hope I'm not opening myself up for more hurt. We'll see though I guess I should get up and go bathe and clean up this house.* Autumn began to get moving but first she thought she needed some smooth groove music to get herself motivated.

"Alexa! Play Sade mix, please." Autumn started cleaning her apartment. As she finished cleaning her room, she decided to move her nest to her bed. It was like a second bed anyway, and why not have a perch? She lit some of her favorite Fall-scented candles because why not. Eventually her whole house smelled of pumpkin spice, cinnamon, frankincense, and crisp autumn breeze.

The scents filled her house with the warmth of her heart and made her feel more like herself again. She felt at peace. *He has ten minutes to show up here,* Autumn thought to herself. She had taken a refreshing eucalyptus shower and dressed in a comfortable but cute t-shirt tank top and a pair of skinny jeans to remind him of what he is in danger of losing. Her hair was up in a curly puff wrapped in her favorite African print. "This is my house and I will be comfortable in it." As her vintage clock struck five, her doorbell rang. *Right on time.* She looked through the peephole and saw him with her favorite flowers.

Okay, breathe. It's just Sabastion. Deep breath. You're still mad at him, though, now answer the door. She opened the door. "Hello, beautiful." Sebastion's smile could melt the polar ice caps. "May I come in?"

She caught herself staring and stopped by answering, "Sure." She stepped aside and he walked in. As he walked past her, she got a whiff of him. He smelled of teakwood and midnight ocean breeze.

Oh, god, he smells like I want to orgasm. No! No! Focus! Stay strong Autumn. You got this. You're still mad. She was having an internal battle. She wanted to walk into his arms and kiss him deeply, because deep down she still loved this man and she had missed him.

"I love your home, Autumn. It reflects you in so many ways. Warm and inviting. Beautifully colorful." Bastion was taking in all of who Autumn was inside her apartment. He knew she loved color, but the way it smelled and actually looked were exactly how he'd pictured them. He loved it. As he was taking in his surroundings, he focused on her.

"You look absolutely gorgeous, Autumn." She was blushing as he stood within an arms-length of her. She didn't need makeup, as her natural beauty was amplified by her freckles and dark-rimmed glasses. *I'd eat her forever*, Bastion thought to himself.

"Thank you. Please come have a seat." She couldn't help but blush and smile.

"Thank you for seeing me and these are for you." He handed her the massive bouquet of flowers.

"Thank you so much. They're beautiful. I'll put these in some water. Would you like some water or something to drink?" she asked over her shoulder.

"No, thank you, I'm good." Bastion watched closely as Autumn walked toward the kitchen. She had the most perfect peachy ass he'd ever seen.

"Ugh" Bastion said under his breath. His pants were getting tight and he had to readjust his position on the couch.

"Are you okay?" Autumn asked as she walked back toward him.

"Yes, thank you." She sat across from him and she smelled delicious. She smelled of honey-suckle flower and orange.

"So you were going to explain everything I missed at the gala events." Bastion began to get upset to be reminded why he was really there. He had forgotten due to his growing need to be inside Autumn. " He took a deep breath and began to unfold everything that happened.

* * *

"We are an hour from the destination, Ms. Catherine. You're sure you don't want me to arrange for a driver to pick you up?"

"I'm good, Charles, thanks." Catherine had been readying herself for this moment. "I'll be driving myself." She had a horrible smile as she placed the razor-sharp knife back in her tactical belt. *Soon*, she mouthed to herself as she sat back in her seat.

* * *

"So you're telling me that I'm an ancient phoenix goddess, and when something traumatic or erotic happens to me, I burst into flames, and grow eagle-sized talons and huge fire wings?"

"Yes. Your eyes also turn this liquid gold molten color and you become ridiculously strong," Autumn laughed a little but sat quietly.

"Have you never wondered why you always run really hot while you sleep? Or why you love the fall scents so much or, better yet, why you feel safest in your nest in your sanctuary of a bedroom looking to the stars?" Bastion asked her. She was starting to connect the dots and her perception of reality was unraveling.

"But mythical creatures like that aren't real are they? I mean … are they?" Autumn looked at him in confusion.

Bastion wanted to ease her frustrations and confusion. "Autumn, my family and I are some of the oldest vampires in the world. We belong to one of the seven houses of oldest lore clans there have ever been. The phoenix and other creatures such as the griffins and dragons were very much real and were supposed to be extinct. But we are learning more and more each day that our kind evolve and adapt to survive."

Sebastion was concerned as he looked into her eyes. "Autumn, do you want me to show you?"

Autumn looked at him in a concerned manner. "Yes." She was nervous, but still steady.

"Do you trust me, Autumn?"

"I do." He got up from the other side of the couch and walked to stand in front of her. She looked up at him and gave a slight smile. He gently took her hand and pulled her close to him, then brought his face close to hers, fangs fully extended and whispered, "Close your eye goddess"

Autumn took a breath and closed her eyes. She could feel the heat of his breath on her lips. He gently ran his fangs over her lips, his fangs ached to pierce her lips.

"Uggggh. Um okay." Bastion gently kissed her lips till her mouth invited his in to her mouth.

He held her close and tight. She stood on her toes to get more of his kiss. "Uggggghhh," she moaned as she kissed him, not of out primal and heated want, but with an unhinged need of him. She needed to feel him between her legs, but more importantly in her life. Her eyes began to change color as her skin began to heat up.

"Sabastion, umm, I'm going to change into something else. These jeans are making me sweat."

He knew what was going on, but she needed to see for herself. "I'll wait here, love." "

"No, I'd like to show you the rest of my house." Autumn was definitely blushing, but it couldn't be seen because her skin was changing to look more rose gold.

"Are you sure?" Bastion asked, wanting this to not be forced or obligation. He was also unable to move very fast, as his member was ready to jump out of his pants.

She began to undress as she walked down her hallway. "Are you coming?" she asked over her shoulder. Bastion jumped up and began to follow his goddess to her temple of secret worship, the sanctuary in which she rests, prays, and prepares to slay the day. So many thoughts ran through his head, as it seemed like they were walking in slow motion to her room.

Once she opened the French doors, Sebastion was in awe. Walking into her space behind her, he found her place to be exactly that, a place to worship this beautiful creature in her natural state of incredible naked beauty. Fire eyes, ocean pussy, she was everything.

She had star-formation tapestries hung behind her headboard with small twinkle lights. She had a floor to ceiling off to the side of her vanity that was decorated with Egyptian hieroglyphics and symbols, as well as golden figurines and other crystals and stars. In the very center of her massive room was a king-sized bed. She had made her nest out of purple, gold, red, and green satin blankets and pillows.

"This is where my beautiful goddess sleeps," Bastion finally said as he again memorized this for the future.

Autumn blushed and smiled confidently, "Yes, I guess. This is where I feel the most peaceful and secluded from the noise of the world. It makes me happy." She loved her bedroom, and if she could live in it forever she would.

She was practically naked, standing off to the side as he observed her room. He turned to find her eyes a piercing golden color to match his own icy blues. Bastion moved closer to her again and took her by the waist. He looked her in those molten gold eyes and whispered, "It's beautiful my love." He felt her body temperature was on the rise to a new heat range. He didn't burn, though. It seemed the warmer she felt the more he was intrigued with her.

"Sebastion," she whispered. "I'm really nervous." Bastion kissed her lips. He could feel her anxiousness, but also smell the jasmine and honeysuckle scent of her pussy.

"Why my goddess?" His eyes were the lightest shade of blue she'd ever seen and she could feel the juices of her pussy running down her thighs and soaking her panties.

Her sweet smell made his member so hard. She could feel him press against her and it made her wetter. "I want to know how you know … I'm a Phoenix goddess or whatever, but I'm nervous about how you'll show me."

Bastion laughed at his almost-naked fire goddess with the utmost love and affection. " Don't be, my love. I always and forever promise to be gentle with you. Always." Bastion was so sincere with his words and actions so far that she felt her walls come crashing down.

"Autumn, I want to show you how special you are, but I also want to show you that I deserve to be the one who worships at and in your garden." Bastion's hand slid around from her waist to her lace pantie line to her soaked pussy print. He took his thumb and began to lightly caress the tiny piece of material separating him from heaven. As Bastion worked his magic on her Pandora's box, she placed her hands on his chest. *He's so built … ugh that feels so good … don't stop*, she thought as she closed her eyes. Her hands unconsciously moved down his to waist and began to explore. They ran up his chest under his shirt this time and Bastion's mind went blank. Her hands were warm to the touch and he welcomed all of it. They were so smooth and inviting. She began to remove his shirt.

"May I undress you?" Autumn asked, looking down as she ran her fingertips across his v taper.

Bastion looked down at his beautiful queen and said in a raspy, breathy voice "Yes, my love, please."

She proceeded to unbuckle and unzip his pants and they fell to the floor. He was partially naked now, and she could see he was very well endowed. *Oh, this thing is huge.* She thought as she bit her lip. Autumn's eyes and mouth were both wide as she gently touched him.

"Uggggh…yes, Autumn." Bastion breathed as he let his head fall back and his eyes close. "Talk to me, Autumn," he finally said, as he wanted more. He moved his hands to her back to unhook the seductive lace skin-colored bralette she wore. It was so enticing, but he controlled himself to not tear that or her panties to shreds. As it fell to the floor, she breathed a deep sigh. Bastion felt her tension rise and fall like her breath and he gently tilted her head up toward his. His sinful smile hypnotized her and gave her a sense of boldness.

She gripped the enormous member with her tiny hand and Bastion almost collapsed. "Oh, god, yes," Bastion said in a deep growl. It was primal and ready for unbridled penetration to the forthcoming ocean excursrion about to happen. She kissed him as she started to slowly stroke him. His eyes slid to the back of his head as he enjoyed this gentle tempting of pleasure. She led him to her nest and had him lay back as she crawled on top of him. Her thighs were hot and sticky like honey was poured over him. She rose and hovered over his almost 10 inches of rock hard dick.

"Bastion, you're so big." Her words almost sounded like a bird's song as she said his name. "I'm so nervous to take you into me."

Bastion gently gripped her hips and said, " I promise to be gentle and so good to you, my love."

Looking into his eyes and seeing his fangs made her even more wet. *How is this even possible?* she thought. She began to slowly descend onto his waiting dick and, as she was sliding down, she felt him pulsate. "Uggggh… Oh Bastion," Autumn breathed.

Bastion's mouth was held wide open as he watched her. He could feel how tight and wet her pussy was and he felt like he would burst if he didn't control his mind. *Breathe Bastion! Fuck!*

he told himself. Her body was now its full rose-gold color and as shimmery as liquid gold. Her body's energy began to form long, visible feathers of flames.

Bastion was sweating from trying not to bust immediately as she began to ride him. "Ugh! Bastion!"

"Oh fuck, yes!" They cried at the same time. Autumn was breathy as she placed her hands on his sweat-beaded chest. Her fingers had transformed into small sharp talons with little black tips. "Ugh. Oh my," she noticed, but couldn't focus from the feeling of him. She began to notice that the more she rode him, the more her body began to glow and the tattoos on her body turned into gold lines that wrapped around her body. She saw the emerging image of herself in her mirror. Bastion could see she was noticing her body change and he took advantage of the moment.

He growled a primal sound to bring her eyes back to his, then held her tight and picked her up. He sat up and placed her on his lap. This time he faced her toward the mirror. "Do you see how beautifully powerful you are, my love?" She began to touch herself as she ground her body into his. She was giving him the ride of both their lives as she watched her image change in the mirror. Harder and harder, she threw it back and finally Bastion couldn't take being gentle anymore. He grabbed her hips once more and this time his own claws were fully extended. He pulled her off of him to lay her on her back as he spread her legs wide.

He pushed his dick into her until he had reached the bottom of her belly. "Ugghhh, Bastion!" she yelled.

"Fuck yes!" he growled as he rocked into her. Harder and deeper he drove into her and she became so much wetter. "Yes my queen, give me all of you!" She arched her back as she fully burst into energy flames. Her eyes were mercury silver, as were his. " His fangs seemed to grow that much longer and sharper and he was looking to make her his forever.

"Bastion, what do you want from me?" she said as breathily as she could muster.

"I want you forever. I love you so much ugh I need to taste you. I need to ugh I must," Bastion said in a deep raspy tone.

She relaxed as he slowed his pace to take himself out of her. He kissed and nipped down her body. The taste of her sweet and spicy skin made his dick that much harder and his mouth water with anticipation. He kissed and left little bite marks on her hips, planning to get back to those later. He kissed her stomach and grazed his fangs against her skin. She shivered as she enjoyed the feel of them. His slid two fingers into her wet sheath.

"Ugh! Bastion!" Bastion smiled into her belly as he licked the sweat beads from her.

"Damn, you are so sweet."

He slid his fingers in and out as to call to her to come to him, and for him.

"Bastion, please don't tease me," Autumn almost begged.

Bastion kissed her inner thighs and nipped at the very edges of her pussy. "Never, my love." As he finished his words, his mouth covered her pussy to give it the most seductive tongue kiss.

"Ugghh! Bastion!" Autumn screamed. Bastion could taste and feel the rush of her juices into his mouth as he drove his tongue deeper into her sheath. She tasted delicious. She tasted of spiced honey and he loved it. Autumn was beginning to shake and she could feel her climax rising.

"Bastion, I'm going to cum." She was breathing hard, as if she was running for her life.

"Not yet, love, not yet." Bastion was drinking from his own personal fountain of youth.

Autumn had been sent from the heavens, and now he was for sure she was sent for him. He was deep in her pussy and he wanted more. His lightly bit her clitoris and that was like the accelerant she needed. She seemed to glow a warm lava color. The taste of her blood and pussy juices was absolutely everything he ever wanted in a lover. He was hooked, addicted, entranced, and in love, fully and completely. As she moaned for more he was rock hard again. He could taste each wave of ecstasy that rolled from her body. He gripped her peachy cheeks and held her to his mouth, not wanting to waste any of her sweet blood and juice. "Bastion! I'm going to cum!" she yelled as she was arched her back.

"Hold on, my love. Let me join you." Bastion brought his mouth up her body and positioned himself again between her legs. He slid into her and again it was like the first time. He almost cried out in ecstasy as he began to rock back and forth. They moved like the moon drives the tide waves of the midnight ocean. They were sweating from the heat of her flames, the heat of their motion, and the energy from their bodies aligning. This is what they needed. Their energies synced as one massive force. It was beautiful. "Can you come for me, my beautiful Nubian queen?"

"Yes, my love."

Bastion's heart almost dropped out of his chest. "Talk to me, goddess." Bastion could barely gather the words. He pulled her close as he drove deeper into her.

He could feel her teetering on the edge of exploding.

"Oh, Bastion! Ugh!. I'm … I'm … cumming."

" Yes my love! Cum for me!"

As Autumn crashed into her orgasmic wall, Bastion was right behind her.

"Uuugghhhh!" Autumn burst into flames as she finally poured what seemed like molten gold all over Bastion. Her bed and her room seemed to have caught fire, but nothing burned.

Bastion growled and finally let go, yelling "Autumn!" as he exploded inside her. They had entered the garden of Eden in each other's eyes. With breaths of pure exhaustion and satisfaction, they looked into each other's eyes. They knew from the look of liquid metal colors they reflected that their happiness was in each other.

Bastion knew Autumn was his happiness. She was his life and forever. She was his beautiful, mythical fire queen. One thought, however, itched the back of his mind as he lay in absolute bliss with his queen. *Would the Lore accept her as the mythical being that she was? They'd have no choice after everything's that's happened.* She was royalty and it was established by a crazy means, but it was revealed. She was his future and he would do anything to keep her safe and happy always.

Bastion's attention was soon drawn back to his current location. He looked down at his beautiful Nubian queen. She was quietly snuggled into him and fast asleep. Her color had returned to the smoothest caramel color and her skin had cooled.

He loved the fuck out of her. As these thoughts ran through his mind, he vaguely heard the sound of the front door being unlocked. *What the fuck was that?* he thought. He was on alert. Something wasn't right, and it didn't feel right in the air. As Bastion slipped out from under Autumn's sleeping body, his senses picked it up. Something was coming … something dangerous. "Noooo!" he whispered, knowing too late what it was. He heard the ticking of the bomb, then felt the rush of air as it exploded. He was knocked out cold.

Autumn was startled awake, only to be knocked out again.

Sabastion found himself blindfolded and tied up when he woke. The blindfold was removed and his eyes went wide.

"Surprise, lover!" Catherine said with a horrendous smile and overall demented look.

"What the hell, Catherine! You're in fucking insane!" Bastion was looking around, trying to gauge where he was and how he could get the upper hand. "Where the fuck are we? Untie me right the fuck now!" Bastion had just realized Autumn was missing. "Where the fuck is Autumn, Catherine?" Catherine laughed out loud and the echo made it sound that much worse.

"Oh, Bastion, sweetie. You ask so many questions," she laughed. "How about some love since I saved you from the clutches of that boring-ass mortal bitch."

Bastion's hatred for Catherine had reached a whole new level. She walked around him, twirling a razor-sharp knife she pulled from her tactical belt. She was completely demented, the literal version of killer beauty. He did notice something off with her hands and face, though. The skin looked uneven or imperfect.

As Bastion struggled to get free, she sat on his lap. "Damn Catherine, get the fuck off me!" She stood up pouting, then in a flash her eyes turned black as she slapped him hard.

"See what you make me do Sebastion?! I don't want to hurt you, but you make me do this to you." Bastion's lip was bleeding but he didn't give in to her. She stood in front of him, hoping for some kind of emotional reaction like he used to give. When she didn't see it, she got even more upset. "Really Sebastion?" She walked away to a small table in the dark warehouse. "Why would I stand by as you waste your immortality on a thing that has one hundredth of your life span?"

She ran up close to him with her knife to his throat and screamed, "I won't!" Catherine's voice echoed through the building like the catacombs of Rome. Her bodyguards were standing by, watching from a distance. She was on a warpath, and they didn't want to be anywhere near it.

Catherine screamed and laughed as she started talking to herself. Sebastion was trying to untie his wrists while she was occupied. He was super pissed she was holding him like this. His fangs were fully extended, as well as his claws.

"I see those scars she gave you haven't humbled your stupid ass."

Catherine stopped what she was doing and immediately touched the grafted skin that covered the most-burned parts of her face. She slammed her hand down on the metal table and screamed again. "You think it's funny, Sebastion?" Catherine turned toward him and asked the question again. "Well do you?" She laughed, loud and angry this time. "I won't ask you again." She smiled in his face and slapped him again. This time he fell to the floor. "Now that's funny!" She laughed as he roared in pain and anger.

"Sebastion, I tire of your games. You be a good vampire and love me." Catherine ran her knife down his chest, cutting him.

"Never, you crazy bitch!"

Catherine stopped and slapped him again. She walked back and forth in front of him frustrated. "I refuse to be second to anybody, Sebastion. Do you understand?" She slapped him again. Now she was breathing hard from being angry. "I'll die before a mortal bitch is better than me!" she screamed in his face again. She backed away. His eyes were obsidian and his claws and fangs seemed to grow even more.

He roared again. "Let me fucking go!"

She spun around, laughing, and pretended to be shocked at hearing those words. "Now, there's no way she could be your fated mate Sebastion, darling, now could she?"

Sabastion looked as hellish as any fully formed vampire in attack mode would. "You're certainly not my mate," he said between gritted teeth.

"Sebastion, why would you say something so hurtful, honey? You're just being a little bitch about our relationship." Sebastion laughed out loud. "You're fucking insane Catherine. Even if we were fated, I'd kill myself before I bonded with you."

Catherine was hurt by that remark. She slapped him again and he snapped at her this time. "Very funny, Sebastion. You bore me."

Catherine was calming herself down. She yelled over her shoulder "Bring her in!"

Autumn was strapped to a chair and gagged, but Sebastion cried out in relief at seeing she was alive. "Autumn! Are you alright?" She nodded as their eyes met, then she was slapped.

"Catherine! Stop this crazy shit!" Sebastion yelled at the top of his lungs.

Catherine was now completely raged out, as her facial skin grafts began to distort. "Shut up!" she screamed "You did this, Sebastion! You shouldn't have rejected me!" She picked up her knife and walked toward Autumn with a distorted smile on her face.

"Gag him now!" she ordered her bodyguards. "He's going to watch me skin his precious mortal like the sweet little animal she is and snap her neck after that."

Sebastion was fighting the guards while they forced him to be gagged.

"Catherine! Don't do this!!!"

"Ugh! Why is he not shutting up?" Catherine yelled at her guards. They finally got him gagged and restrained further.

Catherine got close to Autumn's face and looked at it in disgust. "What in the fuck does he see in you?" Autumn saw this as the perfect opportunity to head butt Catherine in the face. Catherine jumped back, holding her now bloody nose. The guards, as well as Catherine, stood there in shock. The she burst out laughing. "Oh, this is going to be fun." She slapped her across her face again.

Bastion was finally able to get the gag out of his mouth and started thrashing around again. Catherine was clearly becoming frustrated. "What the fuck do I pay you idiots for if you can't keep one fucking vampire restrained?"

A guard punched Sebastion in the stomach, hard, and he buckled. He stilled, then growled at the guard, "I'm going to kill you first."

The guard laughed at him and said, "If you can get out of this chair, you can try, bitch."

As Catherine waited till Sebastion was focused, Autumn realized what was happening and started to squirm and fight.

Catherine hit her again. Sebastion was getting hyped up again and was again punched to keep him still.

Catherine's attention was now back on Autumn. "Hey, stupid bitch." She pulled Autumn's chin up to see her distorted face. "I'm going to kill you for the stunt you pulled at the gala. But first," Catherine sliced across Autumn's chest. Autumn's muffled screams sent Sebastion in to full-on rage mode.

"Damnit Catherine! I'll kill you!"

She turned toward him, Autumn's blood on her face, and screamed, "Not before I kill you first, lover!"

Catherine turned back to her pet project and watched her cries slow down. She was just getting started.

"Why do you think you're better then me? Hmmm?" She put the knife to Autumn's chest as if she was going to plunge it in. Catherine was getting more enraged because Autumn wouldn't answer.

"Answer me!" Catherine screamed in her face, but Autumn was still breathing heavily from the pain.

"Nothing? Fine." Catherine cut her again, this time her arms. As Autumn screamed in pain, Catherine yelled, "I can do this all day, Autumn!"

Autumn's mind was racing. Her worst nightmares were coming true. *This crazy white bitch is obsessed with Sebastion.*

"Answer me! You stupid, useless mortal!" Catherine cut her chest again.

Autumn was bleeding badly now. Sebastion was screaming as he watched Catherine torture Autumn. His eyes crying blood tears as he screamed. "I swear on everything I love Catherine, I'm going to kill you and everything you love."

Catherine laughed out loud again as she watched Sebastion struggle. Finally she walked over to him and slapped him as he jumped around. He was held down by the bodyguards. "Such promises Sebastion …hahaha." She then turned her attention back to Autumn, who had passed out from blood loss.

"Oh no! No, no little bitch. You can't die just yet." As Catherine was about to cut her again, Autumn raised her head. Her eyes were a shimmery gold. Her skin started to glow and ignited into flames.

It was such a burst of light that Catherine backed far away and shielded her eyes to see what it was. Once Catherine's vision had returned, she realized what was happening. She ran full speed toward Autumn to stop the impending transformation. She intended to plunge the knife directly into her chest to stop her cold.

Catherine lunged at her and made contact, then stared as the knife blade melted down to the handle. She jumped back as she witnessed the chains melting and dripping to the floor. As Catherine rushed back in to attack Autumn, this time with a sharp metal pipe, it, too, melted upon impact with her skin. Autumn then pushed Catherine so hard she crashed into the floor across the warehouse.

As Catherine gathered herself among the dust and debris, she saw Autumn stand up and grow the largest fire wings any creature has ever witnessed. The guards, as well as Bastion, were awe struck and terrified at what was happening. Autumn's eyes were glowing lava pools and she flexed black, razor-sharp talons. She finally screamed, a loud hawk-like scream in the midst of her transformation.

While everyone was preoccupied watching Autumn's transformation, Bastion finally managed to get himself free. His sudden freedom startled the guards, but they were fast enough to restrain him again. He sliced the first guard's throat before he could say anything.

"Gotcha, Bitch," Sebastion said as he watched him grab his throat and fall to the floor.

The other guards saw what had happened and looked up to see their fates. Bastion moved like lighting and was on top of each guard in quick succession. "Surprise, Motherfucker!" he yelled as the last of the guards went down. Bastion was covered in blood, but he turned his attention to Autumn and Catherine. Catherine was holding her now-melted skin grafts, which had fallen from her face. She looked at her now boney hands as that skin had melted away also.

Catherine screamed a terrible roar. "I'm going to kill you you fucking freak!" Catherine's boney hands grabbed her pistol and began to empty the clip into the flames. As she shot, the bullets exploded as they neared Autumn's flames.

Autumn screeched and flew toward Catherine. In a flash, Autumn's phoenix form had grabbed Catherine and flew up and out of the building. As Autumn flew, her glowing form could be seem from miles away. Royce and Mira happened to be heading into Bastion's tech building to look for him when they saw her.

"What is that?" Mira yelled. Both her and Royce's mouths hung wide open.

"Oh, shit! That's not good!" Royce yelled. "That's Autumn! Jones!"

Royce and Mira both ran out to the street as Jones was pulling away. "Jones! Wait!"

Jones stopped and they leaped into the backseat. As Autumn flew, she was getting brighter and brighter. "Oh shit, Jones!" Royce said. "Can you ping Bastion's phone to find him?"

Mira, however, was already on it, looking for severely damaged buildings.

"Over there!" Jones, an excellent tactical driver, maneuvered toward the building and they were able to get to it in minutes.

"The ping is saying he's in there," Mira said as they jumped out of the car, ready to fight everybody.

"Who are you? What are you doing here?" Several guards came at Royce and Mira. They hated each other, but nobody threatened them.

"This is what I'm talking about!" Royce went rage mode and so did Mira and Jones.

"We haven't done this in forever," Mira yelled as she tightened her ponytail for the fight. They were fully in attack mode and went to work on the guards. They sliced, slashed, and dismembered until all threats were eliminated.

Mira, Royce, and Jones ran into the building, amped and ready for more.

"Bastion!" Royce yelled as they ran deeper into the warehouse. As they run toward the sounds of fighting, Sebastion was being cornered by some more of Catherine's henchmen.

"Where the fuck do you think you are going?"

"You think you just going to leave here alive, bitch?" the goons laughed as they lunged at him.

Sebastion was exhausted, but wasn't going to die without taking more of them with him. One goon was finally able to grab him and he started to struggle as the others dog piled on him. When he was finally pinned against the wall, the boss walked up to him and punched him in the stomach. Sabastion spit blood out.

"You fucking cost me a client and a lot a men. We're going to enjoy killing a Robertson," the boss said. "Ice this piece of shit," he ordered the remaining goons.

Two goons took out swords and were about to slice him up when Royce, Jones, and Mira appeared in full speed-killing mode.

Together the four made quick work of the remaining goons. When it was over, Bastion fell to the floor exhausted. "Good to see you guys," he said to his family.

"It's good to see you haven't lost your savagery, little bro," Royce said, helping him up.

"Did you guys see Autumn?"

"Yeah man, she was getting really bright as we came to find you."

"Where do you think she's going?" Mira said frantically as she and Jones helped Bastion to the car.

"We have to get to Mount Saint Francois right now!" Jones jumped into the driver's seat and hit the gas, speeding to get to Autumn.

*   *   *

"Put me down, you disgusting freak!" Catherine was now mostly skeleton, as the majority of her skin had burned away. Autumn's phoenix form squeezed her so tight that she screamed in agony. Finally, she dropped Catherine hard on the mountain.

"Where the fuck are we, you stupid bird?"

Autumn screeched so loudly at her in reply that Catherine crawled behind some trees and rocks to not lose her hearing. Autumn began gathering stones, branches, and brush grass into an enormous nest. "I want to leave, you giant fucking dinosaur! Now!" Catherine screamed at the giant fire bird.

Autumn's altered form was tired of Catherine's disrespect and disgusting face. She grew even brighter than before, grabbed Catherine and gripped her tightly, then shot into the sky. Halfway into her ascent she saw others arrive at the top of the mountain.

"Autumn!" Bastion screamed as he watched her fly away. "Autumn! Don't do this! Please!"

Royce and Mira asked in unison. "What's going on? What's she doing?" as they watched her fly higher and get brighter.

Bastion said "She's going to die or kill this form."

"What?!" They cried again in unison.

The beautiful, blazing phoenix cried a single sapphire tear. Where it hit the ground, a dragon's blood tree sprung up in front of them.

Autumn held Catherine tight in her talons as she burst into nuclear flames, incinerating Catherine to nothing but dark ash blown away in wind. Autumn's form sent out a deafening screech as she flamed out and her lifeless body of ash snowed down into the waiting nest.

The nest was enormous, and Bastion climbed into it, finding nothing but ashes inside. He fell to his knees as his brother and sister climbed in behind him. Bastion watched in disbelief as he touched the ashes.

"Autumn, my love." Bastion cried blood tears. "Damnit, Autumn!"

Royce and Mira both knelt beside their brother as they mourned Autumn's death. Autumn was the girl of his dreams, his fantasy, his goddess, and his queen. Bastion was broken. He had lost the one who was fated for him. He bent down and cradled her lifeless, ash-covered body in his bloodstained arms and held her close. He was rocking her when he suddenly stopped.

"Do you hear that?" Royce looked at Mira as if Bastion had lost his mind.

"Bro, Autumn's gone. You saw her burst into flames and hit the ground."

Bastion grabbed Royce's arm and pulled him down to listen for himself. Royce wasn't about to fight his brother right then and thought it best to go along with it.

"Royce did hear very slight breathing. "She's alive."

Bastion looked at Royce and Mira with wide eyes. Mira looked at them and yelled for Jones. "Bring the car ASAP! We have to get Autumn to the hospital, now!"

She was indeed alive, but barely. As they got Autumn into the car, Bastion thought about what his boys from Egypt had said. *When a phoenix needs to rejuvenate, it will set itself on fire and burn itself to death. Three days later, a beautiful new phoenix will be born to start their thousand-year journey anew.*

"Jones!" Bastion said as they were almost to the hospital. "Jones! Go to Autumn's home."

Mira and Royce both looked at him like he was crazy. "Bro! She needs medical attention or she will for real die," Royce said, being the sensible one this time.

"She needs to be surrounded by everything she loves for three undisturbed days to fully heal," Bastion explained.

"How do you know this will even work?" Mira asked, looking as concerned as Royce.

"Please trust me," Bastion said as he held his ash-covered queen.

Once they arrived at Autumn's building they went through her private entrance.

"We can't just leave her like this," Royce said. He and Mira both looked worried about Autumn.

"I'll be here with her," Bastion said. "I love this woman and everything that she is. I would give up my own life to save hers. Instead, she saved me."

"Are you sure, bro?"

"I'm sure. I've never been this sure of anything in my entire life. And that's saying a lot," he replied.

All three of them laughed a little and agreed.

"I love her so much, you guys. I want to be here when she wakes up. I need to be here for us."

Royce gave his brother a hug and held on to him tight. Mira was getting emotional also, and hugged them both.

"Is there anything we can do to make her recoup time more pleasant for the both of you?" Royce asked.

"Yes." He looked at Mira and said, "Since you have my power of attorney, please purchase this building on my behalf."

Mira looked at her brother like he was crazy. "Are you serious?"

"Very much so, big sis. My queen loves this place and it should belong to her outright."

Mira hugged her brother again and assured him it would be done. They hugged one last time, then left him to tend to her.

He laid her more comfortably on her couch and caressed her ashy face. He wanted to be the first person she saw when she was reborn. He got himself settled in and began to care for her.

"Autumn, you are for me. I love you so much," he whispered in her ear.

*   *   *

As Royce and Mira left the building, they glanced up at the high floors. When they got into the car, Jones inquired, "Are we leaving without young Mr. Robertson?"

"Yeah, Jones. He is already home" Mira said.

Royce and Mira smiled at each other as they drove away.

*   *   *

For the next three days, Bastion took the utmost care of her. He took baths with her floating in his arms. He washed, oiled, and brushed her beautiful hair and body. He loved the way his hands smoothed over her body, making sure every curve was delicately taken care of.

Her soft skin and hair made his nature rise. When her skin was fresh and clean from the ashes of her death, he laid her gently in her refreshed nest as she slept and rejuvenated her being. He had bought everything new for her apartment to give her a brand new start. He bought clothes and food for her and some clothes for himself, as he didn't want to leave her side for a second. Jones brought him his work laptop and documents for his daily meetings. For three days, Sebastion was a loving and devoted husband to his queen, the husband he wanted to be. As he finished up some work documents, he sat shirtless in her living room. He was drinking coffee, wearing his reading glasses, his hair in a neat man bun.

He heard the tiniest footstep as Autumn sleepily walked into her living room. Bastion rose and rushed to her, then hugged her and kissed her forehead. She hugged him back and it felt so good. Finally he spoke, "How are you feeling, my love?"

She took a few moments to take in his smell before answering. "I … feel good." She let him go and walked over to where he had been sitting. As he came to sit next to her, he could feel his nature rise. She wore a tiny pair of boy shorts and a crop top and, of course, he loved it.

"Bastion," her voice calling his name broke the hypnotic trance he was in and he responded.

"Yes, my love," he answered in kind of a shock.

"Do I frighten you?"

Sebastion looked at her and felt his heart melt and his pants get tighter. "No, not at all. In fact, it's quite the opposite. I find you very interesting and intriguing."

Autumn seemed to relax a little bit more. "You arouse and excite me," he went on. Autumn's body began to heat up.

"How long was I asleep?"

Bastion cradled her in his arms. "You were out for three days."

She looked shocked. "Wow, no wonder I'm starving."

Bastion burst out laughing and kissed her confused face.

She craved his kisses. "What would you like to eat love? I can have Jones bring you anything you want, anything your heart desires."

Autumn thought about it and Bastion was ready to place her order. "Well I don't think Jones can serve and feed me what I really want." Autumn's eyes grew more golden as she slid her hand between his legs.

Sebastion's head fell back as she stroked the outside of his pants. "So, my lover, could you give me what I need?"

Sebastion quickly turned her on her stomach. He kissed the back of her neck and placed his hands on her hips. She arched her perfect ass up and tempted him to enter her from behind. "Autumn, I've missed the feel of you so much," he said, his rock-hard dick threatening to tear through his pants.

"Make love to me, Bastion," she moaned as her talons grew and tore into her sofa. He slid her panties to the side and brought himself to the edge of her soaking wet, waiting pussy.

"Your pussy is so perfect," he whispered. He slid a finger inside her and she moaned. He began to move it in and out of her, teasing her into short, shallow breaths. He so enjoyed giving her pleasure.

"Bastion, love, I need to feel you inside me."

He loved to hear her say these things. He pulled his finger out as he gripped himself and tasted her nectar. "Fuck! You taste so good. Damn," Bastion said in a hungry growl. His eyes had turned from their normal brownish red to the ice blue. He freed his impatient member and eased himself into her.

He gripped her hips and as he slid deep into her sheath. He could feel every inch of himself being encased by the tight grip she had on him. He had to concentrate to not cum on the first few strokes. She was as watery and deep as the Mediterranean Sea, and he wanted to drown in her.

"Ugggghh, yesss," she purred. Deeper and deeper he slid into her hot, wet center till he couldn't go any farther.

"Wait, my queen. I want to admire the sexy curve of your back."

She began to push back on him and he started to growl. The harder she threw herself back, the deeper into her he plunged. His claws and fangs were fully extended as were her wings and talons. This was love. Sebastion felt the mounting pressure of his orgasm approaching, as did Autumn. Harder … deeper … sweat dripped down his chest and face and pooled in the small of her back.

"Uggghhhh, goddess." He pulled her back into him, still balls deep in her pussy. Her back to his chest, he cupped her perfect breasts as they both started to climax.

"Uuuuggghhhh! Yesss, Bastion!" Autumn screamed. They had missed each other so much, and their journey to each other's stratosphere was sorely needed. They had a truly magical connection, something for the ages. They slowed their pace and finally eased to a stop. She fell softly to the couch, completely drained. Bastion, still breathing heavily, held himself up as if he had just finished running a marathon.

They needed this release, they needed to feel connected, they needed love, ultimately they needed each other. Autumn had regained some strength and wanted to shower.

"We should bathe before we go to bed, love," she said as she maneuvered from under him.

"We?" Sabasation was still recharging from being drained.

"Yes. You and me," Autumn said sweetly. Sebastion rose and followed her to the bathroom. He would follow his queen to the ends of the earth because he absolutely loved her.

"Sebastion, dear…" she said as she turned on the shower.

"Yes, Autumn."

She looked at herself in the floor-to-ceiling mirror and then Sebastion joined her. They were stark naked. She saw him, and he saw her. They were perfect, together. Autumn turned to him and, as gracefully as she could, said "This shower makes me horny as fuck." She smiled a sassy smile and Bastion laughed and grabbed her peachy ass as the entered the shower.

"I love you so much, my vampire love." He kissed her as he lifted her into his arms. "I love you, goddess. Always and forever." They kissed each other deeply as the water poured over their bodies and the steam filled the entire apartment.

The EndTwo years later…

"Honey! Don't you think being on the cover of a tech magazine is a bit much?" Autumn asked, in a playfully jealous tone.

"Not at all. The company has grown so much and is now international, so why not?" Bastion said as he walked into their beautiful new kitchen. "Besides, it shows that the company is run by a person and not a machine." He slapped her plump ass while hugging her from behind and kissed her on her neck.

Sabastion had decided that he wanted Autumn and their future children to live as they deserved. He convinced Autumn to move her practice to New Orleans to manage and live in the ancestral home.

"I don't know how I feel about all those super-smart techie chicks getting off to you, looking all buff and brainy and such." She turned into his chest and wrapped her arms around his neck. She pouted a little, biting her lip, and he found it super cute.

Bastion loved her so much, but wanted her to relax. "My queen, you're the only one who'll get the pleasures they can only fantasize about," Bastion said with that sinfully delicious fanged smile.

"See, when you look like that, I want to get pregnant and trap you," Autumn said, playing with the strings of his sweatpants. She pushed away from him and ran around to the other side of their large island.

"So, you want to play little firebird?" Bastion said as his eyes turned that sexy ice blue and his fangs descended. Autumn laughed out loud and gave him her Come-get-it-Daddy look. Her eyes were golden and her skin began to heat and change.

"I do," she said. Bastion smiled the sexiest fanged smile and, as fast as she blinked he was on her, holding her close by the waist. Autumn screamed out of excitement and true happiness.

He picked her up and placed her on the island top. "Oh, you'll get pregnant for sure. Just know you don't have to trap me, as I am yours forever." They kissed deeply, her thighs becoming wet and sticky. He could smell the honey and jasmine aroma from her pussy as he positioned himself between her legs and it was home to him. "I have something for you, my beautiful goddess." He pulled away from her a little and reached into his pocket. " Autumn Orchiad Scorpeno, I love you and will not accept no for an answer. Will you let me worship at your temple forever?" Sebastion pulled out a tiny purple box from his pocket. He opened it and Autumn's mouth fell open.

"Talk to me Autumn."

She finally looked up and her eyes were the molten gold he loved so much. They made him instantly hard. She was perfect. "Autumn, my love." She took the little box into her tiny hands and just cried. "What's wrong?" Bastion was concerned. "Do you not love it? Was that not what you wanted?" Bastion was stressed out. Royce had helped him pick out the perfect diamond, and he was even looking for something for Sasha. That shocked Bastion, as he would never have thought Royce one to stress over someone until he felt she was his equal and Sasha was it. They were finally back on good terms and were living together.

"Autumn, honey, please." Bastion was on his knees in front of her.

"Sebastion, I love you so much and this is just perfect. I love you so much and oh …" she sobbed.

Bastion was less stressed now and asked. "So is that a yes?" He wanted to be certain.

She sniffed and wiped her face. "Yessssss!" she screamed and jumped down from the island. Bastion laughed out loud, picked his beautiful Nubian queen up off her feet, and kissed her deeply.

When he finally put her down, he slid the ten-carat yellow diamond onto her finger and kissed her hand.

"It's perfect. You're perfect." Sabastion was happy and proud. So was Autumn.

She was so full of life and love and he wanted that feeling forever. As she admired the ring on her finger, a feeling came over her. Giving him the eye again, she said "So, you trying to come celebrate or what?" She playfully bit him and pushed him back as she ran into the living room. She looked back with those golden eyes and he knew he'd chase those eyes, those thighs, and that heart forever.

"Ready or not my love, get ready to cum." Bastion's eyes changed and his fangs descended as he began to chase after his dreams. They were forever wild … together in love.